■ □ ■ □ ■

PAVEL VILIKOVSKÝ

EVER GREEN IS . . .

SELECTED PROSE

Translated from the Slovak and with an introduction
by Charles Sabatos

D1457912

NORTHWESTERN UNIVERSITY PRESS

EVANSTON, ILLINOIS

Northwestern University Press
Evanston, Illinois 60208-4210

Originally published in Slovak under the following titles: *Krutý strojvodca* ("Everything I Know about Central Europeanism"), *Večne je zelený . . .* (*Ever Green Is . . .*), *Kôň na poschodí, slepec vo Vrábl'och* ("A Horse Upstairs, a Blind Man in Vráble"), copyright © 1996 and 1989 by Pavel Vilikovský.
English translation and introduction copyright © 2002 by Charles Sabatos.
Published 2002 by Northwestern University Press.
Printed in the United States of Amer.

10 9 8 7 6 5 4 3 2 1

ISBN 0-8101-1907-2 (cloth)
ISBN 0-8101-1908-0 (paper)

Library of Congress Cataloging-in-Publication Data

Vilikovský, Pavel, 1941–

[Večne je zelený. English]

Ever green is— : selected prose / Pavel Vilikovský ; translated from the Slovak and with an introduction by Charles Sabatos.

p. cm. — (Writings from an unbound Europe)

ISBN 0-8101-1907-2 (cloth) — ISBN 0-8101-1908-0 (paper)

I. Sabatos, Charles. II. Title. III. Series.

PG5439.32.I4 V413 2002

891.8'73—dc21   2001007413

■ □ ■ □ ■

CONTENTS

■ □ ■ □ ■

TRANSLATOR'S ACKNOWLEDGMENTS

This translation would not have been possible without the many hours of proofreading contributed by Dr. Martin Votruba of the University of Pittsburgh and Dr. Zdenka Brodská of the University of Michigan. The help of Pavel Vilikovský (who generously wished me "the greatest freedom possible" in my translation) was also crucial to the final result.

A number of Slovak and Czech friends were kind enough to help me along the way: Mira and Ivan in Bratislava, as well as Martina, Honza, Myron, and Petra in Prague. My relatives in Prešov, especially Lubo and Marian, gave me extensive experience in the spoken language, along with their Slovak hospitality: *d'akujem*. I would like to thank Oğuz for his encouragement and advice on translation, and my family, especially my parents, for their support.

■ □ ■ □ ■

TRANSLATOR'S INTRODUCTION

In the period after Czechoslovakia's "Prague Spring," the work of Czech authors such as Milan Kundera, Miroslav Holub, and Václav Havel gained worldwide acclaim, but writing from Slovakia, the smaller half of the republic, remained virtually unknown. Not a single work of contemporary Slovak fiction appeared in English between the Soviet-led occupation in 1968 and the end of Communism in 1989, and even since Slovakia's independence in 1993, Slovak literature has remained one of the least translated of all European literatures. One of the leading figures of this neglected but promising literary tradition is the novelist and essayist Pavel Vilikovský (born 1941), whose prose displays the same wit and intelligence that has made Czech literature justifiably renowned. One of his stories was included in the 1994 anthology of contemporary East European literature, *Description of a Struggle,* but this is the first full-length translation of his work to appear in English.

Vilikovský's first collection of short stories was published in 1965, but this promising start was temporarily interrupted by the period of "normalization." Unlike many Czech and Slovak writers, he was not exiled or officially banned, but he withheld his own work from the censors for the next twenty years, working instead as an editor and a translator. In 1989, three of his books were released under the quickly weakening Communist regime, including *Ever*

Green Is . . . , which has been described by the British critic Robert B. Pynsent as "a sidesplitting satire on totalitarianism, 'spy mania,' Slovaks and nationalism."[1] In the 1990s, with the appearance of several other works, Vilikovský became widely acknowledged as one of Slovakia's most innovative writers, and in 1997, he received the Vilenica Award for Central European literature.

One recurring element in Vilikovský's prose is his fictional use of historical and literary figures who actually passed through the Czech and Slovak lands, and the story "Everything I Know about Central Europeanism," which first appeared in his 1996 collection *The Cruel Engine-Driver,* describes an imaginary meeting with Albert Camus (who did visit Czechoslovakia in the 1930s). Although it transcends national identities by placing a Slovak narrator in the eastern Czech region of Moravia, the story shows Vilikovský's characteristic ambivalence toward the idea of "Central Europe."

The impossibility of publishing his work gave Vilikovský greater scope for imagination in the title novel *Ever Green Is . . .* , perhaps his most challenging and rewarding text. The aging narrator, a nearly senile spy, overwhelms his listener with a constant flow of information of dubious accuracy: sometimes he craftily alters the truth; sometimes he simply forgets it. The story also bears testimony to a generation of East Europeans who eagerly learned everything they could (from the limited, sometimes inaccurate books available) about countries they would probably never be able to visit. Timothy Beasley-Murray of the University of London has argued provocatively that the novel "makes use of a radical postmodernism of resistance, rather than the reactionary postmodernism we are accustomed to in the West."[2] Beginning as a spy novel in late-Habsburg Central Europe, it crosses borders of geography and genre, relentlessly satirizing the national, political, and cultural assumptions of the late Communist era with its linguistic playfulness. *Ever Green Is . . .* has also given me the possibility of testing the boundaries of translation; in one or two instances, I have tried to exploit the limitations and possibilities of a translated text in order to show the reader the intended connotations of the original.

"A Horse Upstairs, a Blind Man in Vráble," which was also first published in 1989, demonstrates the author's versatility with its more introspective, sensitive style. Yet it shares some of the same concerns with language, memory, and society that appear in the other works. In her review of the French translation, which appeared in 1996, Pearl-Angelika Lee praised the author's "extraordinary sense of humanity and humor."[3]

As one of Slovakia's leading translators of British and American literature, Pavel Vilikovský has brought such authors as William Faulkner and Virginia Woolf to Slovak readers; I am pleased to have the opportunity to return the favor.

· · ·

Notes

1. Robert Pynsent, *Reader's Encyclopedia of East European Literature* (New York: HarperCollins, 1995), p. 429.

2. Timothy Beasley-Murray, "Postmodernism of Resistance in Central Europe: Pavel Vilikovský's Večne je zelený . . . ," *Slavic and East European Review* 76, no. 2 (April 1998): 268.

3. Pearl-Angelika Lee, *World Literature Today* (Winter 1998): 181.

■ □ ■ □ ■

EVER GREEN IS . . .

■ □ ■ □ ■

EVERYTHING I KNOW ABOUT CENTRAL EUROPEANISM

(WITH A LITTLE FRIENDLY HELP FROM OLOMOUC AND CAMUS)

> Central Europeanism is not a state citizenship
> but a view of the world.
>
> *György Konrád*

A MAN CAN SPEND HIS WHOLE LIFE IN CENTRAL EUROPE without necessarily being a Central European. In the mountains of Slovakia, I've met men who are absolute sovereigns of their territory, that is, the land which they cross with their own feet. They know on which path they might encounter a bear, where they can pick medicinal agrimony blossoms, and when to go down to buy fresh bread. It's strange that in big cities and big villages, these people move very hesitantly and speak disparagingly and indiscriminately about them. Perhaps it's because those places are so dirty. Their healthy common sense suddenly and sorrowfully fails; it doesn't express an experience, only a mood. ("But you see, that is very Central European!" as Camus might have told me. "Can a person possibly arrive at a more precise experience than a mood? Even the theory of relativity is an idea of genius only because Einstein was able to express his mood in a mathematical formula.")

Well, and then a man can be a Central European his whole life without ever finding that out. I had the good luck to meet Camus at the main train station in Brno.

It may come as a surprise to those doing research on Camus's *Notebooks* that he passed through Brno in his wanderings. His *Notebooks* don't mention his visit to Olomouc, and today I am certainly the only one who knows about it. Camus is dead, and the desk clerk at the Palace Hotel has also died since then, sometime at the beginning of the 1980s. By a coincidence which I don't have time to relate now, after many years I became better acquainted with the desk clerk. He was an educated man who had an ardent relationship with literature. In fact, he wrote science fiction stories, full of fantastic creatures like J. R. R. Tolkien's. As far as I know, not a single one of them was ever published. ("How Central European!" Camus would have certainly said.) One way or another, that educated man with literary inclinations showed no signs of surprise when he wrote the name "Camus" in the guest book. I'm just mentioning this as a little excuse for myself.

At the time, Moravia was having its day in the sun. It was sloped so delightfully that some future European writers flowed down to it, pulled by gravitation, while others actually sprang up in it. I think that at some point during that time, Jean Genet was locked up in the prison in Ostrava for theft and loitering. He'd gone to visit his Polish lover and trickled down to Ostrava. He didn't get any further; they sent him straight home from there.

So Camus was traveling incognito. What else could he really do? If he had started to shout in the Brno train station *"Je suis Camus!"* people wouldn't have thought that he was Camus, but that he was a madman. Certainly, no one is a prophet in his own land, but even if nobody gives a damn about you in your own land, it doesn't necessarily mean you'll be considered a prophet somewhere else.

No, there wasn't anything striking about Camus. Maybe I actually noticed him because he blended in so well with the Brno station. If he had intentionally looked for a suitable background, he couldn't have chosen a better one. Such a sedimentary, ingrained sadness, all the reasons for which had long since gone away, like the soot on the rails of the electric track. I didn't think he was on that bench waiting for a train; he didn't look like a passenger, but like a person on a journey, and it somehow had no connection with the station. He would have looked just the same in the foyer of the Janáček Theater. A man of whom two of his friends say behind his back, "He won't be with us much longer." Fine, just as long as he doesn't get bored, my dears!

As I said, Camus didn't make any kind of exotic impression. He had a slightly darker complexion, but there are some faces that simply darken from fatigue. Faces—pockets under God's eyes, which announce that God has had a bad night. Black, closely trimmed hair, a cigarette hanging rakishly from one corner of his mouth—but who wouldn't know Camus's photographs? With that suntanned complexion he looked a little bit like a Sicilian peasant, although I had never seen a Sicilian peasant. Speaking for myself, I would rather say that he was sad, but lively, even joyfully so; he was at home in that sadness, in his element. His eyes jumped like the seconds on a digital watch.

At the time, I was young and still believed in coincidence. I thought that this man had really come up to me to light a cigarette; we'd exchange a few words and somehow begin to appreciate each other. Now I guess that he'd already given his eyes their fair share, and had decided to progress to the next stage. Listening. He scrutinized me and thought I'd make a good stool pigeon.

As for myself, I have a special relationship to Brno. It's the only city in all of Moravia, and Bohemia for that matter, where my father died. I mean to say that I grant Brno certain privileges, and—let's render unto Freud, who also emerged from the Moravian soil, what is Freud's—every time I have the opportunity, I walk through the streets around the station in the secret hope that my father will come around the corner, see me, and say: "So here I am." And I'd tell him: "It took you long enough." It would be just his style; why, he even went to die in Brno without saying a proper good-bye. He just told us in the kitchen, under the lamp, "Well, see you later," and then we saw his reflection for the last time in the windowpane. Incidentally, after so many years I certainly wouldn't have recognized him anymore. Black, closely trimmed hair, a cigarette hanging rakishly from one corner of his mouth, fingers yellowed from smoking . . . why not?

Various minor things played a role: for example, that Camus was a foreigner, which was a relatively rare bird in our geographical latitudes back then. Here it wasn't just me personally at stake; I stood for all the others—so that he might take from us, if nothing else, a good impression. Not that I would have directly given myself such a task, but it fluttered somewhere in the back of my mind. ("How charmingly Central European!" Camus certainly would have said.) Well, and there was also, actually, the foreign language. A person can say things in a foreign language that he would never find himself saying in his mother tongue; the person speaking the foreign language is also foreign, and he doesn't feel any responsibility or shame. It's like painting by numbers; everything important is decided in advance and all you have to do is avoid painting outside the lines. So much freedom!

At the time, my actual destination was Olomouc, where I had to serve on the jury of—if I'm not mistaken—the Miss People's Democracy Pageant. There was a direct train from Bratislava to Olomouc, but given my special relationship to Brno, I thought that I'd interrupt my trip and visit the Brno Exhibition Center, where a furniture trade show was just taking place. Truth be told, the one who thought of it was my wife, who was still young and believed in the future; in particular, she believed that the time would come someday when we would have our own apartment. As a rule, I only pay attention to moments when they're present, but it was no trouble for me to pretend a little for my wife's sake, especially when I knew beforehand that we wouldn't be buying any furniture. And I dumped all this down on Camus, breathlessly and topsy-turvy, because in my heart of hearts, I was worried the whole time—he was French, had a rakishly hanging cigarette, and so on—that he would ask me where to find a whore in this town. I didn't know, and what was worse, at that time I wouldn't have recognized a whore even if we had bumped right into one.

Naturally, after so many years, I can't reconstruct our conversation word for word. In fact, it was hardly a conversation at all; Camus simply picked my brain (he himself formulated it in a more considerate way, that he "wanted to support his opinion with my experiences"). But at the time, I didn't realize that. I remember he asked me why I was so skeptical about furniture, and I told him that in our country, what you see on display in a shop window you can never find in the shops. In our geographical latitudes, a shop window is not an advertisement, but a conditional mood, that notorious "if only," and the sales clerk's role is not to sell, but to explain why we can't all be in heaven. So in that case as well, my skepticism showed itself to be fully justified; the set of furniture I was interested in was sold out for the next two years and they didn't take orders for the next shipment.

He liked that; not, I guess, what I said, or how I said it, but I think it pleased him, the way he figured me out, how exactly I suited his purpose. It was humbling, actually, if I had realized it, but I didn't poke around in his approval. I felt a jolt, and that was all I needed.

"If a person goes out on that stage that stands for the world," I said—the foreign language had already grabbed me by the throat and was dragging me wherever it wanted to—"then he looks around, to figure out where he should move to. Well, in our geographical latitudes, it's enough if you turn your attention to something personal for a moment, like tying your shoelaces, and when you lift your head, you find out that in the meantime the scenery has completely changed. So in our geographical latitudes, you not only can't buy furniture, you can't even produce it three years in advance."

"That's good," laughed Camus. "In your geographic latitudes? Do you mean Central Europe?"

I didn't mean Central Europe, since until then I had never encountered that concept, not even on the weather forecast. What do they mean by Central Europe, when with all the curtains around it, you can't see past your own barn! No, "our geographical latitudes" was a code name, an unobjectionable term for a certain social system—or establishment, as they liked to say in those days. I'd warrant that Camus would have cried, "That's a downright Central European approach, to call a regime a 'geographical latitude'!" if he'd been informed of that, but you weren't supposed to blurt out such things to a foreigner. So I just nodded.

That's how it was. Just prattle, the same trifles and poppycock, but it really seemed as if Camus was irresistibly drawn to it. As if his interest were directed by a standpoint of meaninglessness; as if only the meaningless had meaning for him. He was, if I can put it like this, a historian of that which had no history, of the crumbs that had fallen unnoticed under the table of history. Was it possible that he could experience only those homeless, uninventoried moments as life? These days, now that we have so many meanings that they are starting to lack reality for us, these days I think I understand him. My God, how I hate history, that autobiography of humankind! But it's possible that Camus's interest in the trivial was just a way not to be pulled out of his thoughts.

"In America," he said, for example, "where these contests were actually invented, they have pageants for the title of Miss Sprained Ankle, Miss Roundest Belly Button, or maybe Miss Birthmark on the Derrière. There the criteria are more or less clear. But Miss People's Democracy?"

I tried to explain to him that in our geographical latitudes, even in beauty pageants we don't consider a woman

EVER GREEN IS . . .

an object, a conglomerate of more or less accidental, though eye-pleasing, shapes. It's not a matter of conferring a prize for design, or taking the exact measurements of some Annie or Mary or other. When a woman turns out well, she embodies for us not only herself but also something else, something higher. For that very reason, the organizers had invited several writers to be on the jury, because they were the greatest experts on spiritual values.

"A remarkably Central European attitude," Camus remarked. "But it actually means a big success for you!"

In a dignified, perhaps even somewhat touchy manner, I answered that I couldn't consider that a success, because I don't know about either women or highest values, and even if I did, I haven't had the opportunity yet to demonstrate my own eventual knowledge, so the organizers chose me for irrational reasons that were quite incomprehensible to me. Besides, being on a jury had never been one of my ambitions. That is, I don't leave my goals to be determined by outside forces—I determine them myself, so I'm also the only arbiter of my successes.

"From what I hear, you're not going to enjoy a lot of success," Camus said, and compared my situation to Sisyphus, who painfully rolled a boulder up a hill, just to have it always roll back down just before he reached the top. With the carefree pessimism of a young man, I said that, I was no different in this respect from the rest of mankind. If we consider how many possibilities a newborn baby has before it, and how few of them have been fulfilled at its death, we can, with a clear conscience, call it a fiasco. And it took off from there. According to Camus, the Americans, for example (now that we've mentioned them), would try to make the dull boulder-rolling more exciting with a contest for the person who could roll it the highest, and just before the moment that the boulder rolled down, they'd take a picture of it as proof. "In our geographical latitudes, where we're particular about certainties,"

I answered, "Sisyphus would have carried the boulder down the hill on his shoulder, so it wouldn't roll away anywhere, because what are you supposed to do with the rest of your life without a boulder to roll up the hill?" So we just continued our silly chatter, and I didn't even realize that Camus—due perhaps only to his absentmind-edness—had come into the compartment with me. The train started off.

Moravia, where I know it, flows by slowly, and from behind the train window it seems stickily sweet. Like honey. It stuck my mouth shut. In Olomouc, I had a room reserved at the Palace Hotel. Camus joined me. "*Voulez-vous coucher avec moi?*" I asked him, a little clumsily, but he got his own room; he must have found the blush that soon suffused my cheeks unbearably Central European.

Early in the morning, before breakfast, we went for a little walk. We kept walking straight ahead, so we wouldn't get lost. We were surrounded by houses that were black in the morning mist. Plaster drizzled down silently.

"A sad town," I said, when the silence started to oppress me. I thought that I'd fit in with Camus's mood, those brown hues, but he corrected me: "It's a town where it's rained for a long time." He lifted the collar on his jacket and his moist eyelashes bent down like ripe ears of wheat. "It remembers, but it doesn't feel the need to talk about it," he added. "And that's what it's all about: remaining the master of one's own defeat." After that, we went on through the sharp air in silence.

I guessed that by traveling, Camus was trying to solve a problem, or at least looking for a setting where his problem wouldn't be so striking. It's always the same problem, it just has different names in each period of time; these days they've nicknamed it the "identity crisis." I'd say that his girlfriend had left him; a whole series of tormented ques-tions are usually released in a young man on that occasion, from "What doesn't she like about me?" all the way up to

"Who am I, really?" That direct hit to the solar plexus, solar nexus, or solar sexus, when we find out for the first time that we seem different to others than we do to ourselves! In vain the naked Romeo feels limb after limb, to figure out what is the Montague in him; in vain behind another window, the naked Juliet looks in the mirror to figure out what is the Capulet in her! But it doesn't matter; even if he cut off and cast away everything in himself that he recognized as Montague, after that cruel dismemberment he would only face another, even harder question: What is the Romeo in me? But the solution is entirely simple and Gordian. I think it was most beautifully expressed by György Konrád, even with a tiny drop of amazement under his nose: "I have actually discovered that everyone is always only one."

We elected the Miss People's Democracy, but that didn't solve much; a year later it was necessary to pick a new one. It was just that a year later one of the writers from the jury was in America, another one in Canada, and a third in France. With my clumsiness, it took me longer, but at last I too found myself abroad; these days another European writer, who was born in Moravia but wandered only as far as Prague, is speaking not only of them but also of me when he says: "What bothers me so much about those émigrés is that they consider themselves more valuable people than the rest of us. As if they were the only ones deserving to be rescued. If there were freedom here, they certainly would have stayed. So yes to freedom, but no to a mass grave? Who do they think they are?"

When I went back to the hotel in the evening, the desk clerk informed me that Mr. Camus had vacated his room and departed. I never met him again. The memories become thinner, the bare body of life starts to shine through at the elbows and knees. There were moments that I thought I had dreamed it. No, he doesn't mention Olomouc in his *Notebooks,* but years later, I found a similar town in one of his novels:

"It's true that nothing is more common these days than to see people working from morning till night and then choosing to waste the time they have left for life by playing cards, going to cafés, or chatting. But there are still towns and countries where people occasionally feel that there are other things in life. It usually doesn't change their life. But at least they've had that feeling, and that always means something."

That is Camus's bequest to Olomouc, or perhaps also Olomouc's bequest to Camus. One way or the other, we can certainly agree that it is essentially Central European.

■ □ ■ □ ■

EVER GREEN IS . . .

1

Beginnings, you say, first steps? How good-looking I was then! A pale face, that was the fashion, velvety blond whiskers . . . yes, I still didn't shave much; that was when I became the lover of Colonel Alfredl.

You know this case, of course, but you know it in a completely different way. I don't claim that I remember all the details, it's already . . . nine and two is sixteen, sixty-one years? All roads are open to a young person . . . in the case at hand, so as not to exaggerate, at least two. After all, at the time I still didn't focus on women—I only acquired this vice later, during active duty, and the colonel was not responsible for that at all.

When they told me then: In the highest interest of the homeland, in the name of the holiest Christian traditions, personified in the imperial and royal crown . . . K.u.K. himself summoned me; that's what we called him, the chief of the third—or was it fifth?—three and five, of the eighth department. He stood with his back to the door; the Venetian blinds were down . . . they went down automatically, just by pressing the knob on the door; but it was harder—just between us—when it came to pulling them back up.

In a word, K.u.K. himself . . . pronounce it as if it were one word, "kook"; you don't really read the periods, of

9 + 2 = 16

K.u.K.

course—at the periods you just let your voice drop. One doesn't remember everything, but basic things, like for example letting your voice drop, they stay with you. It was a division of the intelligence department . . . but I already said that. "Dear boy," that's how he always addressed me when there were just the two of us; he caught me around the neck in a friendly way, he stood quite close to me, I could tell how the hairs quivered in his nose, and he felt my shoulder with his hand. I used to have strong shoulders . . . feel them, yes, even now, just feel them. I was exercising according to the Sandow method.

scurvy

The famous strongman Eugene Sandow, as you probably don't know, was a weakling who, from his birth, suffered from rickets, syphilis, scurvy, hay fever, I can't even remember all of his afflictions anymore. His classmates, you know how children are, made fun of him . . . did you happen to read about it? I don't want to waste any time. . . . Then he started to exercise, and one day he picked up the teacher, along with the platform and the blackboard, with his left hand. On top of that, of course, you'd have to see how well nourished the teachers were in those days . . . civil servants, with pension. It was in math class, I remember it as if it were yesterday. . . . Now that was a good book.

taming
sensuality

To tame sensuality means to withstand temptation. I'm making it a bit vulgar. Take it as a poetic abbreviation. To love a man . . . is he perhaps an inferior being? From the standpoint of value, as such? But that's just by the by. The first thing was to unlearn love, except, of course, the highest kind, love of an idea. Between us, it's like sucking a thumb, or at worst a big toe.

The room was filled with the delicate scent of Katharsis perfume (I'm now referring to another room, not to the intelligence department office); the walls covered in red leather glittered scarlet like an open wound.

"Colonel," I exclaimed, "listen to a wretched being!" "Take heed of" may sound better, but I would use that only to communicate with God. The feeling that invested in these words, which burst out from the open soul of a growing youth like pure water from a spring . . . that youth was me, at least back then I was in the bud of youth, and open despair caused my otherwise pale face to blush. There wasn't a dry eye in the house. He had two of them; in that sense he was normal. The glass in his monocle flickered with a hot metal glitter; it was, as you certainly anticipate, bulletproof. not a dry eye

"Colonel," my words rang out, marked with deep emotion, "take heed of . . . I want to say, listen to a miserable man. I have long resisted the feelings which develop confusion in my soul and pull me in two; me, who as long as I can remember . . ."

"Hold it," the colonel said, with a single commanding gesture of a hand accustomed to giving orders. He had delicate hands with long manicured fingernails and a big gold ring on the little finger of the left hand. "The punishment for treason is death." Now where were we? The hand lightly landed on my shoulder and under its searching touch, with the exciting hint of an understanding, I noticed a strange similarity. You might call it a coincidence, but it was too amazing for the thought (which at the first moment seemed almost like blasphemy to me) not to fly through my head. The hand that weighed upon my shoulder . . . they later gave me 300 crowns at the pawnshop for that ring, and it's worth remembering that in those days you could still get a good pair of shoes for 10 crowns. A kilo of good-quality pork lard cost 3 crowns . . . or 7? Seven and three, seventy-three. In many countries seven is considered a lucky number. the punishment for treason 1 kg = 3 Kcs

"Before we come to the matter which, as I can see, presses heavily upon your heart—" and as the colonel said those words, he lightly put his delicate fingers on the place where that most human of all muscles was beating with excitement under my blue silk shirt. I don't mean the one that you're thinking of, I'm speaking of the one up here on the left. "So first of all," the colonel continued with the the most human muscle tender smile that stood between me and his actual thoughts like a flimsy, albeit opaque, curtain, "let us divest ourselves of these formal garments which remind us too strikingly of our social rank and obligations, and allow me to lead you to my parlor and offer you a light snack, such as the austere abode of a bachelor might happen to offer."

With these words he led me deeper into his apartment, furnished even by the standards of that time with unusual, even startling, luxury.

"I see, young friend," said the colonel and, smiling, pointed at the empirical, or rather, Empire settee, covered with violet brocade, "I can see that you are surprised to find this—let me be a little immodest—sophisticated taste and elegance in the home of a rough soldier, a man who has

the rattle of weapons spent his whole life in the rattle of weapons."

An impartial observer at that moment probably would have called his smile ironic. If he had squeezed into the apartment, of course, through the carefully locked doors, which had closed silently behind me, thanks to a Brano auto-

Brano closes doors matic door closer. "Brano closes doors automatically," as the ads used to say in the days of the bourgeois republic, my friend—have you ever seen one? Then the colonel just needed to turn the large key, completely inconspicuously. . . . The left hand doesn't know what the right is doing.

I say an impartial observer, because how could I consider myself an impartial observer, I who against my will was gazing spellbound at the classic Roman profile of the man sitting across from me, the profile which abundantly fulfilled the promise of the frontal view? Under his nose he had a wart with three little hairs; in our profession we cultivate a sense of detail. Of course, I was still just a beginner then, but

genius let's say a talented beginner. Genius is 10 percent talent and 90 percent hard work. I was, it's no longer necessary to hide it, nearly a genius; and I might add that the word "nearly"— do you sense it?—is there as a purely stylistic decoration.

"A concession to conventions, my dear Colonel," I said, when I turned off the lamp with the pink lace shade. The ambiguity of the situation—because no doubt, I thought when I felt how his hand glided over the smooth velvet of my body, that squeeze, that searching touch of body to body, hesitant for a moment, then hungrier and greedier, which I had felt recently, recently and in very strange circumstances, which were already fixed in my memory. . . . It was—as you have already guessed, young friend, because surely you know the classic rule of storytelling: when Chekhov had a gun in his first sentence, it was fired in his last one (an eloquent testimony to the quality of weapons back then)—it was, as I said, in the deep darkness behind the doors of the eighth department, and that man, whose loud breathing I felt next to my ear, was none other than the great K.u.K. himself, who had given me the top-secret mission of carefully watching him in the form of Colonel Alfredl. At that moment I could not understand the ambiguity of that situation other than as a certain form of trial, the most difficult trial, on which depended the whole rest of my life. Chekhov

I accepted; without a single shudder or hesitation I took up the gauntlet; and in that game, the rules of which I did not know—what is more, the rules of which intentionally had to remain a mystery to me until the end—I decided to create my own rules. In a word, I told myself, they won't outsmart me. I did not permit the colonel's hot embrace to obscure my thinking for even a moment. The body, of course, should be given what it needs; between us, it's like when you suck your thumb. As long as you don't have any problem with breathing—and you don't look like it—five minutes later you forget all about it. Where were we then? Oh yes, on the settee in the pink parlor. taking up the gauntlet

2

Dear young friend, I see traces of inner confusion on your face, a certain, I would say, moral quandary. Your sympathies for a young, talented, and keen-witted officer, not entirely dissimilar to yourself—well, my ears did not stick out so much, and as for your nose (are you Jewish?)—are struggling with disgust at the situation, which was a denial of life's conventions and traditional morals, not to mention good taste. Although taste . . . good taste, if I may reveal to you one of my personal experiences, good taste is a curb on social progress. I could reply to you in the words of the old the gates poet who wrote on the gates of hell: "Abandon all hope." of hell Abandon all prejudices, all conventions, those who enter one of the most difficult professions, the profession which . . . because in this case it's not really a profession, but a calling, as they used to say, not a job that you can perform routinely, without your heart in it, eight hours and that's enough, back to the family circle, to indulge in your hobbies. (I have never in my life, for example, been to a soccer match.) It's a calling that requires all of your energies and abilities, and the reward? The only reward is your awareness of having been a part of historical motion, the midwife, so to speak, of historical change. Because, remember, all changes that become a part of history are historical.

Well, the only reward, so when I say only, I really mean it—well, you do make a little something here and there, but those are more or less the costs of maintenance; all that alcohol . . . maintenance is naturally more expensive for sophisticated mechanisms—really, the single reward is the awareness that you have helped to turn the wheel of history; to the left or the right, that's all the same, the main thing is whether it moves. That is the higher morality above ordinary scruples. You're a cricket of history, of course you know it. *Arbeit macht frei*—which is the only freedom for people like us. Even in those most intimate moments, in the deepest privacy . . . but, as our double-dealing colleague Admiral Canaris would say, my deepest Canaris privacy is a state secret; and remember, that applies to every major figure in our line of business.

When I say "in the deepest privacy"—like now, for example: "in the deepest privacy of the pink salon"—I'm making use of an established cliché, rather than exactly expressing the real state of affairs. So in the privacy of the pink salon, between the soft clouds of cushions—good, isn't it? the fluffy flock of cushions—and now you . . . what, you give up?—in the foamy surf of cushions—and again you . . . you surrender?—in the cool waves of cushions . . . in the fool's cave of cushions . . . yes, while the colonel sank lower and lower on the slippery slope of physical desires the steep slope and the movements of his hands lost the last remnants of of desire imperiousness, I saw, in spite of the darkness, which was illuminated only by the flame of flaring passion, my unenviable situation quite clearly. I was a toy in the hands of a doubled-sided individual, who in one of his disguises was misusing me for the satisfaction of his admittedly understandable, but not completely natural, appetites, but in his other role, under the mask of my superior, he received all of my news and reports about his own ego, and personally rendered them harmless. The vicious circle that had me in its grip was really hermetic. Even in case I could have decided to increase my pocket money with blackmail, with what could I have threatened him? That I would have reported him to himself, hidden in the artificial darkness of the eighth department? And later, nothing would have been easier for him than to wipe me out early, inconspicuously and—let's say it openly—completely.

Perhaps someone else in my position would have helplessly given in to his fate and striven to find the better side of it; but I, in spite of my unripe age, was a young man of penetrating intellect and judgment. . . . I'll give you a word problem, all right? The distance between stations A A, B, C and B is exactly the same as the distance between stations A and C. Got it? The question stands: Do all three stations lie on the same line? Ha-ha.

Now, where were we? Yes, the colonel had his weak-
crotch nesses; he was a crotchety man: and then his hand with the soft long fingers, as if electricity was flowing through them, lightly glided across my crotch, searching for the hard spot . . . no, that's not what I wanted to say. Let me put it like this: Not yielding to the passions which I cleverly and convincingly simulated, I searched feverishly in my mind for the colonel's soft spot. Between us, he was ticklish, but that wasn't what I wanted to say . . . although that sweet little detail humanized him somehow in my eyes; the threat of the situation lost its thorn. Do you understand that? I don't very much, not anymore. In short, it had to do with finding his vulnerable place, his Achilles' heel, as they say.

In the dusk of the salon my thoughts flew about like frightened bats. Like sparrows when you shoot at them. Although if I shot at sparrows myself, they wouldn't fly around anymore, I can guarantee that; this hand. . . . Don't be misled by this slight trembling. The weight of a pistol multiplied by the length of an arm divided by two. A hundred points out of a possible ninety. I don't want to seem as if I'm boasting, but in the thin Alpine air . . . while you were shooting, you had to pay attention, so a sudden step back didn't put you off-balance . . . one morning, from a distance of fifty meters, I knocked down, what was his name . . . the Matterhorn, no, that's the name of the mountain, not the man. The mighty beauty of the Alpine cliffs, yes, superhuman in their ancientness, inhuman in their cold; the bells of Swiss mountain goats were ringing out faintly. . . . They got my goat, those stubborn Swiss
Sextett heretics. His name was Hazi Schwarzwald Sextett; I knew I'd remember his name. Among friends, and in a way I could count myself among his friends, he was called Sexterli.

After all, it can be said of the person who sends us to the other world that he was in intimate contact with us. I can't imagine anything more intimate. Against the sky rise the magnificent Alpine peaks . . . they don't rise, but once they rose. Oh, sky-high! Just remembering it awakens the poet in me.

Mont Blanc is precisely 4,807 meters high, but those are the Savoy Alps. The Matterhorn is only 4,505 meters high, but it's so steep! The Swiss president's name is Little Peter—Petitpierre. The greatest reserves of gold are hidden in the vaults of Swiss banks, and that is exactly what concerned us. The Swiss franc is divided into 100 centimes, also called *rappen* in German. Visitors from Europe can bring 200 cigarettes, 50 cigars, or 250 grams of tobacco. Do you smoke? Smoking is a part of disguise. Fifty cigars!—carrying coals to Newcastle, as they say. . . .

Mont Blanc

"Dear Colonel," I said, gently shaking off his meticulously tended hand, "we gave in to a feeling, which we could, considering how quickly it flared up, call a momentary . . ."

"Proof!" exclaimed the colonel. "My friend, so you ask for proof! As if you didn't have eyes, as if they didn't see, as if they saw and refused to believe! A form of proof, you say, and a convincing one! As if each word, each movement of the hand, each breath of a trembling chest . . ."

The colonel stood up and began to pace around the room with brisk steps. It was, if you're interested, four meters twenty in length. The Persian carpet muffled his steps like grass; the hand-knitted skeins parted gently. . . . During the official evaluation of his estate, they assessed that carpet at 872 guilders, and if the colonel hadn't paced so often and so resolutely, it might have been even more.

4.2 m

"Proof!" the colonel continued, and when I unsuccessfully tried to object: "Let's not talk about it anymore. . . ." He silenced me with a single gesture of his hand. It was a hand which did not brook any opposition, a hand which decided on the lives of tens of thousands of people with a single gesture. If I wanted to impress you, but I don't care for effect, I could easily have said hundreds of thousands and I wouldn't have been far wrong. I'm seldom wrong, my dear friend, but if it does happen, it happens in a big way. It means that my mistakes become landmarks of history. My mistakes! If they could have been predicted, I would have held the future of humanity, so to speak, in these hands . . . yesterday they didn't shake so much. Pour some more.

"A form of proof," the colonel continued, "and a convincing one! As if a sincere feeling needed any proof other than the crystal tinkle of its own echo! As if there existed anything more tangible, more concrete than . . ." An eloquent fellow, wouldn't you say? In spite of the dark thoughts that were feverishly flying through my head, I could not help admiring him in a part of my mind. But with the second part, and in that rested the essence of my unusual talent, I was already thinking of how to turn this apparent advantage to the colonel's disadvantage, how to make use of it professionally. Professionally speaking, an under-the-threshold thought. Nearly all great thoughts have been born under the threshold. The theory of relativity, for example, when Einstein was a petty paper-pusher—a tax clerk, in a word—he burned away his brilliance at the revenue service in Bern. All in all, the theory of relativity is just a harmless joke, a rebus, but let's take, for example, the five principles of extinguishing forest fires! Let's take Ludolf's number, also known as pi, or Madame Bovary—who was, incidentally, a Hungarian Jewish woman by origin. You can object, and essentially I agree with you, that it's a decadent book; but remember the right-hand rule in the Highway Code or, if you like, the Marconi-Popov wireless transmitter. Now come up with something yourself. Pasteur was walking in the woods when he was attacked by a dog infected with rabies . . . and, back in Colonel Alfredl's embrace, I came up with an idea as simple as the egg that Columbus crushed to make it stand on end. I was truly on the ball . . . to be specific, the lower one, on the left.

I don't know if you realize that in view of its weight, the left testicle is the bearer of fertility and virility; thus even people with one testicle, on the condition that it is the left one, can retain an undiminished capacity to reproduce. And they may even produce identical twins, who grow from a single egg—that's having your egg in one basket, so to speak. One well-known historical figure, after an unsuccessful attempt at a putsch in 1923, stumbled while trying to escape, and his friend Röhm stepped on his scrotum with an iron boot. But let's leave that between us. Other than me, the only person who knows about that is his personal physician, Dr. Hanussen, who (as a forensic pathologist ascertained, when they found his corpse in the gutter next to the road) had died of chicken pox. I have it firsthand, from this very hand . . . that's funny, yesterday it didn't shake so much. Pour some more.   chicken pox

I sat, and I'm speaking confidentially, with the above-mentioned individual in a cell in the Landsberg prison, and given his inclinations, which were not completely out of keeping with my own youthful thoughtlessness. . . . Nowhere does homosexuality blossom as in prisons. Incidentally, I contributed to his premature autobiography more than one of my stimulating ideas . . . thoughts . . . I see: so I came upon the thought which, even if it couldn't be implemented immediately, gave me a clear perspective, a goal to which I could devote my full effort.

"Dear Colonel," I said in a voice suddenly noticeably colder, in a voice in which an insult was trembling, "I wasn't thinking of a tangible proof that would please a low soul with material goods, a proof that honest people would call a bribe; but if you are so jealous of proofs of your favor that you give preference to gross humiliation, that you open the dams of your eloquence, only in order to . . ."

"Enough!" said the colonel, and at the sound of his voice, the folds in the pillow timidly smoothed themselves out; the starched shirtfronts that had been hurriedly cast away under the pressure of passion seemed to rustle nervously. "Enough!" The hand lifted up, imperiously covered my open mouth, and pushed the word that was being born in it back into the womb . . . the throat, the womb of sounds—good, isn't it?—the womb of meaningful sounds.

3

Well, well, dear young friend! You say that not all sounds born in the throat are meaningful? Well, well! Don't reveal in front of an expert that you give in to the first, most superficial impression! Of course, I don't deny the first impression its advantages: a certain universality, inaccuracy, stemming from the awareness of the universe . . . yes, the first impression is the treble clef of the still unwritten symphony of knowledge. I must even admit that in our profession, we are dependent many a time on first impressions, because time does not permit us to wait for a second one, to say nothing about the possibility of verifying the truth. Ultimately, truth is only a working hypothesis. A true man does not seek truth, a true man simply creates it—he forges it, he forces it on reality. And as my life draws to a close, even with my proverbial modesty, I feel entitled to call myself a true man.

Precisely because of this, young friend, believe me when I say that each sound that comes from the throat is meaningful. Only my advanced age and, I confess, a certain contempt for these kinds of activities prevent me from compiling a four-volume encyclopedic dictionary of nonverbal sounds; so it's not a lack of knowledge, because, I tell you without boasting, I knew all of it, and in the open countryside—not like you, who have only seen a few examples molting their feathers in the cage of literature. Good, isn't it? In the rusty cage of literature.

An expert can take a sound, which comes from the throat seemingly by chance, even against one's will, and deduce not only the sex and age of the sound producer, not only the character and quality of the experience that forced it out of him or her, but also the time of year and atmospheric conditions at the moment when it was made. For example, the gunshot on the Matterhorn with which I sealed the fate of Hazi Schwarzwald Sextett. Haven't I told you about that yet? Then I have to. It was a beautiful plan: how to break apart the bastion of banking, and make a little profit at the same time. Switzerland, that is, Schweizerische Eidgenossen-schaft, or as the French say, Confédération Suisse, does not have any colonies; ultimately they would have been good for nothing anyway, since in 1958 alone, the Swiss made 38 million watches. Let me see, that is—according to the 1957 census—seven watches per inhabitant, while in India peo- 7 watches per ple were starving . . . the only clocks accessible to the pop- inhabitant ulation at large were sundials, not to mention the rainy season. How would a simple Indian family cook their soft-boiled eggs for breakfast? From this point of view, it is sheer luck that a simple Indian family never gets any eggs at all. In Hindi, therefore, there is no special word for *vyklepok* *vyklepok* (those cracked eggs sold half priced in Slovak groceries): a clear consequence of their long years of colonial bondage. The same fact, namely the lack of an English equivalent, is on the contrary a consequence of the long years of their colonial supremacy. Those are the laws of dialectics; I could have explained it to you in greater detail, but we would have digressed; enough about that. . . . Now, where were we?

"Enough!" cried Hazi Schwarzwald, holding on to a protruding rock with one hand, and his face was disfigured by . . . His face, frankly speaking, was difficult to disfigure; it was even in times of sweetest sleep the very death mask of Beelzebub. When Hazi began with his dangerous pro- Beelzebub fession, plastic surgery was still in diapers. We could say that a whole generation of now world-famous Swiss surgeons has grown up on Hazi, and first and foremost on his face. Which, as I have already mentioned, at that moment was disfigured by a triumphant grin. "Enough," he cried in a powerful voice and the enormous stone face of the mountain multiplied his words, "not another step! A single movement—and I should mention that a single movement in this situation would not help you at all; you would need a whole series of them—but as I say, a single movement is enough, and it will be your last!"

I was looking directly at him during these words, but I admit that the only thing I saw was the barrel of his pistol, which was aiming directly at my chest. My situation was, even in the most optimistic estimation—but in all of my actions I held on to the principle: Estimate pessimistically, act optimistically; after all, there is something optimistic to overcome in the very act of acting . . . it's exalting to overcome circum-circumstances stances—in a word, my situation was hopeless. With the nails of my right hand—they were longer; I did not acquire that vice of biting my nails until my years of well-deserved retirement—I convulsively sank the nails of my right hand into the ice-covered crust of the snow, so I could save my body from falling into the depths. In those days the Mat-4,505 m terhorn was 4,505 meters high. In my left hand I was grasp-ing a released pistol; yes, it was really the left hand, and my target was in a safe hiding place behind the protruding rock, and what was barely sticking out from behind it? Yes, I already mentioned that . . . the barrel of his pistol. You're not paying attention!

Frankly speaking, a little bit of his goiter stuck out too. The Swiss wear goiters the way other nations wear folk costumes, and Hazi had a big one. Did they take it from the Saint Bernards, or was it the other way around? In short, Saint Bernards wear a little barrel with rum around their iodine necks, and the Swiss a goiter with iodine. Swiss water is poor in iodine, so the Swiss have to carry it with them. But even if I had managed to hit him . . . I have always shot worse

with my left hand; it is well known that left-handed people are mentally deviant, didn't you know that? Even if I
had hit him, the bullet would have flown smoothly through
the tissue and except for the opening, from which iodine
would have flowed, it would not have left any damage.

"Hazi!" I responded in a voice under whose seemingly
calm surface a powerful current of resignation could be felt
(I made sure of that). "A single movement, do you say, sir?"
(We addressed each other formally in contact on official contact on
lines.) "If I make a single movement, a bullet from your official lines
pistol would be useless; it would hit only air, for at that
moment my body would already be falling powerlessly
into the bottomless ravine."

As I was saying those words, my left hand got a better grip
on the handle of the pistol and my raised index finger strained
to cock it. It was, naturally, at that moment more of a reflex
than a well-thought-out operation, more of a predeath spasm
or blind determination rather than a purposeful attempt to
put up resistance in a situation which even a layman would layman
certainly have called hopeless. But that is precisely why he
would be a layman. Perhaps it could even be said that the
harder the task, the more it awakens ambition.

All of this, naturally, Hazi did not anticipate at that
moment. He didn't know, because he couldn't, how the
weight of my whole body was transferred to my right foot
and to my hand, now so steadfastly (if not sled-fastly) fastened
in the crevices of the crust of snow. And simultaneous with
the sound of the shot, I slid down from the projecting rock
with my left hand and hung above the yawning gullet of
the abyss.

Eeeeooft, and here, finally, we have reached our topic:
Eeeeooft, the bullet whistled melodically in the thin air of
the Swiss Alps. If this same scene had taken place in a fertile
green valley among silently ruminating herds of cows . . .
but first of all, the Swiss would have had to raise another
breed; Simmentals are known for noisily chewing their Simmentals

cud . . . regardless, in other geographical latitudes and especially other elevations above sea level, that same sound would have to be called a whizzing—*shooeeeest*—can you hear the difference?

I know what you'll say: That sound did not come from a human throat, but that's just the beginning. *Bghraugh!* thundered a burst of gunpowder just after the bullet, repeated a hundredfold by the echo . . . a hundredfold, most likely you understand, I say only because it's a round number; actually the echo did not repeat more than seventy-three times . . . well, seventy-four at the most.

Hazi, a native Swiss, was naturally prepared for every eventuality, including a climb of the Matterhorn, and therefore he had a high-mountain silencer installed on his pistol; but I—why keep it secret?—did it completely unrestrainedly and without the appropriate consideration. When *plop!* I heard the quiet *plop!* as if the beaks of two crows had bumped into each other, I was already hanging in safety behind the rocky massif. In safety, perhaps, only in the sense that one death is safer than another. And even before I had found, feeling at random, firm support for my feet, at some distance strange sounds were heard, at first only muffled: *kledly-klak, kladlay-klik.* . . . With eyes wide open in amazement, I stared at the little tumbling pebbles, which were loosened under the huge, seventy-three-times-multiplied *ghudlaghag* sound of my shot; one, then another, ten, *ghudlaghag,* the sound got deeper as the stones increased, as suddenly a rolling loosened mass fell thundering into the valley, and here we are: *krroukhlokh* came the desperate groan of the struck man, and although my view was blocked by the split peaks of the cliffs, from that strangled sound I was able to deduce everything that had happened; even in advance I had already guessed the final blunt stroke which put a full stop on the long and productive life of Hazi Schwarzwald Sextett, whose friends, if such a monster can have friends at all, called him *dzhbuech* Sexterli: *dzhbuech!*

Yes, dear friend, on the basis of a single sound I saw before my inner eye the death of a fifty-nine-year-old man, who was slightly hoarse—this was caused by that uneconomical conversation with his expected victim, that is, with me: the air was admittedly thin, but sharp—as he was buried in a huge, growing rocky avalanche, thanks to which . . . but that's another story . . . a flourishing quarry arose at the foot of the Matterhorn. To this day I receive thank-you letters and Christmas greetings from the townsfolk there. I don't want to exaggerate my role, but I did solve, at least within the framework of one canton, for many years to come, the problem of Swiss emigration: the well-known Gastarbeiters, as they called the impoverished *gastarbeitr* classes of Swiss citizens who had to go abroad to earn their daily bread, disappeared into the dustbin of history. So no wonder that the Swiss president Little Peter, or Petitpierre, a direct descendant of William Tell, not so much in sharpshooting, but rather in the devaluation of apples, bestowed upon me a Medal of Merit.

You say, at least you could, that my analysis of sounds remained completely on the surface, but even here the explanation is at hand: Our time is limited; therefore, as you must have already noticed—provided that your youthful egocentrism allows you to notice anything besides your- egocentrism self—I'm telling this simple story in a straightforward manner, without any kind of ornamentation or digression. But at least let me offer you a glance into the wide gardens of acoustics, and as an example, let's use the sound which we can spell out as *bghraugh!* In this agglomerate of sounds, the sound *b* expresses the volume of the cavity from which the sound emerges. Since it is a variable, *b* may sound rougher and more barrellike at one time—for example, look at my huge chest—and duller and less sonorous at another time, as it was in the case of that sickly Hazi Schwarzwald Sextett. *G* expresses the explosiveness of sound; its quality is constant, but its quantity changes in direct proportion to *b*. *H* indicates the air conditions, the amount of resistance which the air or other obstacle puts up to the penetration of the sound. The quality of the sound also changes according to the size of the resistance, whereupon the most frequent variant is *kh*, or the sound indicated phonetically by the Greek letter *gamma*, and popularly

glottis called a glottal stop; here, naturally, *glottis*, like *scrotum*, is just a Latin term for that part of the human body that directly . . . am I boring you? It seemed to me that you were dozing off.

Good, I see that the fine nuances of acoustics have so far eluded you; I don't dare to judge whether you lack merely a proper education and adequate training, or whether you don't even meet the basic standard, that is, you don't have talent. After all, this does not change the fact that, as long as I call the sounds coming from Colonel Alfredl's throat "meaningful," you have no grounds to argue with me. Who was there, you or I? Who responded, with a silent shake of the head, to the colonel's ungrounded accusations, which were more emphatic with every second?

"Enough!" exclaimed the colonel, for the umpteenth time . . . my specialty was word problems; simple addition and subtraction did not have enough charm for me . . . and the hand that was covering my mouth pressed down with even greater weight. He always sprinkled two drops

Herbicide of the cologne Herbicide into his palm; I have a strongly developed sense of smell and, each time, I recall . . .

"No one can doubt my generosity," rang out the colonel's proud words, in which there was, if you listened carefully . . . and one of my principles was always to listen carefully . . . in which there was more pride and vanity than sheer feeling. It is naturally better for national security if men in leading positions do not succumb to sheer feeling. There's nothing for which people commit more dirty deeds than for sheer feeling. I'm not speaking of myself; I always had enough antibodies. I only want to say that what the tone

of the colonel's voice gave away did not surprise me at all;
if I relied on something sheer in our relationship, it was
sheer sensuality. Why should I conceal that back then I
was as beautiful as a cherub. Have you ever seen a cherub?   cherub
That's what I thought. . . . How to explain it to you, since
decorative epithets would only give a mere hint of the
overall effect of my gentle, touching, shy beauty, to which
we tiptoe in silent regard. . . . Now try it yourself. If you
can't, close your eyes for a moment.

Oh, let's drop it! I am not going to keep it secret,
because the ardor with which I'm speaking about it gives
me away: Yes, I couldn't help falling in love with myself.
In sensual, I would even say physical, love. A look at
myself, frankly speaking, did not evoke anything good in
me. The lowest instincts. When I stood naked before the
mirror . . . and now the colonel's thirsty eyes served me as
a mirror. Or rather, his hungry eyes. Appeasing hunger is   hungry eyes
a longer procedure, but then again, thirst is more excruci-
ating. But both of them, and this is the basic thing, are
satiated by gulping greedily. There is no more appropriate
word to describe the colonel's look at that moment, when
he drew a circle around himself with a broad gesture of
the hand that he had removed from my mouth. I understood immediately that it was not only a symbol of everything that surrounded us in that cozy but rather feminine
room—it represented the whole world.

Yes, dear friend, the colonel's look was greedy; and I,
who was not only beautiful but also smart, could not but
draw my own conclusions: I would have certainly been a
tasty morsel for this powerful and lustful man, but at that
moment I was already strongly determined that if I were
going to serve as nourishment, it would be only in the form
of hors d'oeuvres, which, as is well known, stir up rather
than satiate the appetite. The details, if you happen to be
interested, can be found in the book *Cold Quick Meals* by
Winter and Krembholz; a very useful little work. It's not

only up to date but it also records the phases of historical development, from the oldest quick meals to the present.

I must admit, good food is one of my weaknesses. Like our line of work in general, good food is a part of disguise. A person who always eats scrambled eggs in order to save *History* on traveling expenses cannot intervene in History with a capital *H*. I understood this right at the beginning of my professional career, and without a tremor in my voice, without a flicker of my eyelids, I replied to the colonel: "Even though our unique relationship . . ." In Switzerland, for example, just so I don't forget, there are three cuisines alongside each other: French in Valais, Vaud, and Jura, Ital- *St. Gotthard* ian south of the Saint Gotthard Pass, and German in the rest of it. To prepare their famous fondue, you need an earthen or stone pot, which you carefully rub with a clove of garlic; then pour in half a liter of white wine and add seventy-five dekagrams of Gruyère cheese, cut into thin pieces, add spices and mustard, and warm on a low flame, mixing everything with a wooden spoon, until the food gains a creamy texture. Then we add a gill of cherry brandy and serve it right in the pot, into which the feasters dip pieces of bread stuck on forks. *Bon appétit!*

4

Do you have a handkerchief? You're drooling—not there, on the left corner of your mouth—that's it. It seems to *fantasy* me, young man, that you have an excessively lively imagination. An unfortunate phrase, by the way, an excessively lively imagination. Something's either alive or dead. Of course, you don't say of imagination that it is dead, and if you did, I could not claim on the basis of my own experience that the imagination of a man in our line of business should be dead; it should be rather unconscious . . . so that you could revive it at a suitable moment, but so that it does not hinder your performing your duties.

Imagination, if you allow me such a comparison, should be like a life-size rubber doll, which you can freely inflate or deflate . . . but who now, among us, inflates a life-size rubber doll? I made use of that worn-out trick—you know what I have in mind: an inanimate substitute—only once, and my pursuers caught me dead tired in the middle of inflating a dummy, which should have taken my place in the bed. To deceive an adversary, it is enough to leave the water running in the bathroom, not very hard, just dripping, and hang your socks on the radiator; but be careful, not washed socks . . . it's strange, when I think of how much time our people spend washing socks in hotels, if they don't want to catch athlete's foot . . . in a word, it's enough if the colleague on the other side has a vivid imagination; if not, he sees . . . what I mean is, he just smells the socks, just hears the water; but if he makes the mistake, which we learned to avoid a long time ago, and loosens the bridle—do you hear how well those words express the nature of imagination?—if he loosens the bridle of imagination, right away he hears a person breathing in the room. Is your breath bad? Sometimes it's caused by chronic tonsillitis. As the German slogan puts it: *Odol beseitigt den Mundgeruch.* Odol mouthwash makes bad breath go away. And it does indeed. The colonel had the most beautiful two rows of teeth I have ever seen in my life, and those two white rows twinkled milkily in a rigid smile, when I repeated, but this time don't interrupt me, please:

"Even though our unique relationship, of that I am sure, dear Colonel, cannot be understood by the conventional souls blinded by prejudice, among whom we are destined to mix, nevertheless, my sheer delight in your company, not entirely unlike the feeling of a faithful wife who follows her husband wherever the winds of fate may blow him"—I believe that the comparison of fate to the wind is quite truthful, and more often than not it is a strong north wind—"commands me. . . ." Are you following

dummy

Odol

north wind

me? I'm not speaking of the colonel, even if his curt words sounded many times like orders; I am speaking of the sheer delight. ". . . commands me, dear Colonel, to express the desire which in other circumstances I would perhaps consider too bold."

I couldn't help noticing, since the upper half of the colonel's body was not covered by any garment, how, upon hearing these words, he instinctively strained every muscle . . . let's speak openly, between men: I don't know about all of them, I don't even know if it was instinctively . . . and yet the seeming untruth of those words conceals another, deeper truth, as you have certainly, my dear friend, understood . . . you haven't understood shit, "but I don't want to give up the hope that one day, one beautiful day, you will understand, dear Colonel, that every little moment I can stay with you, respectfully following from bustle afar your charming manly figure, shining in the bustle of everyday life like a star. . . ." It's funny, as a child I thought that a starlet was a baby star and couldn't understand why my uncle said all starlets were whores . . . how admirable are the paths of a language. If a bee finds a good meadow for honey, it communicates it through a special dance. The chimpanzee belonging to the Kellogg couple could answer the question "Do you want some orange?" He answered with an affirmative sound of assent. You are as many people as the languages you speak. Do you want some orange? I don't have one anyway. A parrot can even learn the Apostles' Creed and rattle it off, "I-be-lieve-in-God-the-Fa-ther-al-might-y," not, of course, with great piety, rather jerkily, but you can understand it. Do you believe in God? Religion is the opium of the masses. Dogs still bark the way they did in the past. Lassie comes home. My Sultan didn't come home. Another victim of the silent, never-ending war. The Frenchman Faguet wrote chiffre about the word *chiffre:* "The word *chiffre* is rough; it illustrates well the feelings that numerals arouse." And it was a

Slovak linguist who answered succinctly and readily, in a book published by Ján Trnovský of Nové Mesto nad Váhom, in his own print shop and at his own expense, and let me say that he spoke for me too, answered: "Rough? The heck it is. The word *chiffre* is as innocent as an angel. The roughness that Faguet attributes to it comes from bills, especially when they are big and we can't pay them." Dry numbers and paragraphs always evoke dread and aversion in politically minded people. paragraphs

But I wouldn't like to get bogged down in a fruitless language dispute. When linguists can't come to an agreement, the state has the final authority. How much trouble and time would have been uselessly wasted in Germany on the question of whether to write in Gothic or roman letters, how much paper would have been uselessly spoiled! And nothing would have come of it as a result. The Führer Führer decreed for them to write in roman—it's a known fact that Gothic letters caused difficulties for him—and the arguments ceased. You see, a nice example of the role of the individual in history.

The German word *Herr,* "mister," comes from the old *heriro,* which was the title of the noble lord, on whom a person's existence depended. The *Frau* was his wife, at that time a lady of high station. These days any vagabond vagabond is a *Herr* and any beggarwoman a *Frau.* While begging and door-to-door peddling are forbidden in Germany, the shallow happiness of a well-fed burgher can't hide the complete decline of German society. Using that premise and thinking logically, we reach the conclusion that a hungry peasant's happiness is deep. From that point of view, we are all creators of our own happiness. The mass migration to cities is one of the mechanical consequences of the scientific-technological revolution. New York has 13 million inhabitants, including the suburban areas. In the times when it was still called New Amsterdam . . . but let's New not be sentimental. Amsterdam

"Let's not be sentimental, dear Colonel," I said hastily, in order to relieve the tension that was showing in the colonel's entire being, "but on the other hand, let's not forcibly suppress the sheer feelings that bloomed in the warm atmosphere of that precious moment, but could easily be burned by the frost of alienation."

"Alienation!" cried the colonel, and he feverishly started to feel around with his hands. "When I hear the word 'alienation,' I reach for my pistol!"

Fortunately—as I don't even need to tell you, because otherwise I wouldn't be sitting here with you today—fortunately the colonel, in anticipation of amorous games, had long since unbuckled the holster with his pistol and, in a moment of flaring sensations, had tossed it on the settee.

shoot! "Shoot!" I then said calmly. "And until the day you die, be tormented with the realization that"—between us, if the colonel had been tormented by anything, it would have been only with the realization that he hadn't had more fun with me before my death—"be tormented with the realization that you have destroyed an innocent person, devoted to you, before allowing him to utter the words of love. Because what else to call the request that you should allow me to be near you, completely inconspicuously, only as one of the many who surround you in the busy moments of your life filled with productive work? What else to call"—you know, I really knew how to bamboozle him—"this modest request but an expression of sincere devotion? What else . . ." Admit it, my dear sissy friend, what else? Don't be such a sissy; try a little! Blow up—this is a suitable moment—the rubber doll of imagination, let it grow to its full life size! Let it proudly thrust out its sunken chest, let it menacingly move its until-now paralyzed limbs! A declaration of love, you say? You call that imagination? That's a dead canary. Let's drop that.

"What else?" replied the colonel, and pay attention now, because that was a different format. "What else? If all of these circumstances were not so absurd, if you were not so much at the mercy of my favor or disfavor, I would simply call it blackmail. This way, however, not mistaking the quickness of your judgment for its depth, I will wait a little while before calling it anything, and give you the opportunity to demonstrate that you have not resorted to words of sincere devotion out of calculation or cunning, but only because they express reality."

While he spoke these words, and it was not necessary to look at a stopwatch to ascertain that it took him quite a while, the colonel came closer to me, put his manicured hands on my still-bare shoulders, and when he lowered his voice to put a period on the sentence, he also lowered his head to the soft little hollow that was etched above my collarbone. That little hollow, I should add, had as sweet and irresistible an effect as a dimple; but unlike the latter, it had the advantage that while a dimple only appears during a smile, and so frequently forces the person who relies upon it for effect to smile idiotically and without any reason, the one above the collarbone is, so to speak, everlasting. Should I undress? Even today. . . . Well, all right, then.

The effect of those little hollows is so powerful, the spell of innocence and childish charm so captivating and convincing, that many of our male and especially female colleagues did not hesitate to undergo an operation, only in order to decorate the cheeks with them, as well as (such examples are known too) other parts of the body. Mata Hari herself had one such irresistible little hollow in a place which we usually show only to the family doctor. At the same time, it also explains why she appeared in most of her productions in the nude or covered with only a thin veil which could be torn off at any moment by a well-timed gust of wind. But I can tell you, and I say this to you man to man—although I would hardly call you a man, but for your sake perhaps we won't correct our proverbs and sayings, not to mention comparisons . . . have you noticed that the second part of a comparison always has wider latitude, contents, and more life than the first part? For example: You smell like Napoleon after the Russian campaign. How much action is in it, how much space, the wide Russian steppes—and you? You are, and not only in this comparison, nothing. Now it's your turn, and if you respond to my attack with an attack of your own, I'll tell you in advance that I won't feel offended. I caw like a crow? Stale, my dear friend, and mistaken; you certainly don't know that as a boy I sang in a choir and my angelic voice . . . all right. Now my turn, and in order to show you my virtuosity, I'll begin from the same starting point: You smell like broth from the socks of an Olympic marathon champion. Good, isn't it? Your turn. Yes, yes. I smell like shit, that's true. Admirable. Sharp and to the point. One point I envy you, I admit: that flight of fancy.

Napoleon [margin note]

Olympic champion [margin note]

Let's drop it. We've digressed and it wasn't even worth it. I wanted to tell you, as one man to another, but now I'll tell you just like this: I was one . . . I almost said "of the few," but that would have grossly distorted history. Not that history doesn't need or couldn't stand some retouching. Only a primitive serves meat raw. I actually admit proudly that I myself have often served as the paintbrush with which a nobler or more powerful hand smoothed the rough lines of history, but it always took place in the name of a higher idea, and not because of some whore, if you'll pardon the vulgarity.

So I was one of the mortals, the many mortals, who had the chance to see that little hollow, that little punctuation mark of beauty at close range. That little valley! That delightful region surrounding it! One was the decoration of the other, one addressed the other with the most beautiful names. A person would not even dare to interrupt the conversation, in order not to blaspheme. Do you believe in God? Religion is the opium of the masses. Opium is the religion of the masses. Thus speaks the iron

That little valley! [margin note]

law of dialectics. The peculiarity of that little hollow, and that was the essence of Mata Hari's fabulous performance, was the fact that when Mata Hari smiled with her lower lips . . . and have no doubt that she knew how to smile with them; they smiled, I would almost say, of their own accord, like when a mushroom picker says lovingly of mushrooms, "They just smiled at me from the thicket." They had their own life, their own truth; and in vain the upper lips wrinkled in a furious grimace, the lower ones, with a welcoming—and that is quite a weak word—smile, proved they were lying. Do you know Latting's scale of smiles? It is scientifically proven that the human face can make 243 expressions in a single minute; in the case of trained individuals, such as actors, barbers, tavern-keepers, and hysterics, as many as 372, and if by coincidence the categories overlap, such as hysterical barbers, we can double that figure. But why should we do it, even if we knew how to? My strong point was word problems. Did you ever fail a grade in school and have to repeat it? A person in our line of business shouldn't avoid any kind of experience.

But I really wanted to say that if you got angry with the upper Mata Hari, you could still be fine with the lower one. I was personally fine with her up to the moment when the bullet of the firing squad put out the life in both of them. What a pity. The human body still has its limits. That upper one, she really knew how to get on someone's nerves, let me tell you. If I want to preserve a good memory of Mata, each time I have to repeat to myself that the true, the real Mata Hari, her better—much better, believe me—ego resided from the waist down. Poor girl. In her mad midlife infatuation, she thought that she could tug me into the harbor of marriage. That delusion of hers acquired a perseverant form. She wanted to set up a workshop for me to repair bicycles and sewing machines. I was supposed to make the warranty repairs for Singer. But a person who has once stood on the stage, those boards that

Latting

better ego

stand for the world. . . . In the Middle Ages they imagined the world as a board that was carried on the back of a whale giant whale. Perhaps you'd ask, as I would, why a whale should carry a board, when we know well that a board floats by itself; the whale, however—you mustn't forget that we are dealing with the darkest Middle Ages—is in this conception of the world none other than God. Do you believe in God? At that time they did. The globe, as we imagine it today, is also just a working hypothesis. It was all caused by that lunatic who stumbled upon the meridian in Greenwich. It was just a periodic phenome- Halley's non, like Halley's comet, for example . . . but the delusion comet which pursued Mata Hari and with which, in turn, she pursued me was not, unfortunately, periodic. What other choice did I have but to pass along those few documents, which were worthless, by the way, from a historical point of view, but unusually attractive from the point of view of war hysteria? After the war she could no longer live by dancing, that much was certain; at the most she could elephant perhaps join the circus as an elephant woman . . . she was woman already getting flat feet from obesity. All right, but to become the wife of a bicycle repairman? From this you see, my dear friend, that she had already lost the last inhi- bitions; ultimately there was also that incident with the fur coat. . . . The execution was staged and everything could have ended with her health certificate and police registra- tion being withdrawn, if Mattie (as, being on intimate terms with her—and having every right to be—I called her) had not at the decisive moment spread open her fur coat. Dyed rabbit, if you are interested in the details. They say that she didn't have anything on under it; but only a blind man could call those enormous volumes, not sup- ported by any undergarments, nothing. . . . But one should speak only good of the dead. Enough to say that for greater trustworthiness the firing squad also included a certain recruit, who (in mortal fright) forgot his orders when the fur coat was spread open, and instinctively shot straight into the silent—at least in that moment, in that single moment—the silent menace.

A sad tale, and instructive. The saddest part is that together with that already worn-out body was also extinguished that charming little dimple, which . . . eh . . . each time . . . cough, cough . . . each time, when . . . cough . . . cough, cough lend me that handkerchief. A real man is not ashamed of tears, but I can't stand it when my nose is dripping.

5

Well, now I've had my catharsis. Pain cleanses. Pain is, if one can speak indelicately of delicate things, the diarrhea of the soul. That's why pain is so unbearable for people with no spirit: in their case it is, so to speak, senseless. Pain is the secret door to the universe. . . . Do you believe in God? Modern skepticism is alien to me. Religion is the opium of the masses.

Pain is like sandpaper, with which you scrape the every- sandpaper day dirt away from yourself. . . . I don't mean the situation when your hand gets slammed in the door of a tram; pain like that does not elevate you, and if it does, then it's only from one tram stop to the next. What I have in mind is a moment of quiet pain, which could also be called sympathy, over the corpse of an old enemy! What a superficial feeling, by the way, is friendship in comparison with faith- faithful ful enmity! I say "faithful," because I'm not thinking of the enmity enmities that arise purely from a surplus of temperament and die away at the first knocked-out tooth, when a chaotic mind wins a point that it can hold on to. Faithful enmity, a relationship charged, so to speak, with its own dynamo! All tensions and sparks! In our line of work one hand washes the other, and thus perhaps it is useless. But when you're standing over the corpse of your old enemy, especially if it's one whom you've sent to the next world by your own hand, you feel as if you've just come out of a cleansing sauna. You don't go to the sauna? I knew you weren't the type to throw away ten crowns just like that, for nothing.

Naturally, I don't have in mind the false sentimentality that prevents you from searching his pockets and removing a gold necklace with a cross, the sentimentality that forces you to search in your mind for the long-forgotten words of a prayer, with hypocritically folded arms; no, nothing cheap . . . not shutting his eyes, which in either case no longer see nor are curious about anything, which do not widen in astonishment at the sight of you trying on the corpse's terrycloth socks. . . . It's not hygienic, by the way. I'm thinking, rather, of the feeling of gratitude toward the deceased that is born in your heart, conveniently colored by the surrounding scenery. Take some-

Savoy Alps thing like the Savoy Alps, the sky-high peaks of the mountains which touch the stars—on the assumption that you were lucky enough to get a direct hit in a clear summer night—and the stars bump into each other with a quiet little clink; on the left, across the sky, the thick cream of the Milky Way. . . .

Now, what were we talking about? Oh, yes, surroundings; naturally, not only like a frame on a picture. They say, for example, death in Rome. A well-known work, and not the only one. To a hysterical individual, it seems as if a death in such a setting gains in meaning, as if he became greater in his own eyes. You know that sudden desire at the end of life to add a greater meaning to one's existence; the very word "add" means that it is something additional,

P.S. post scriptum, after the empty meaningless rambling, a convulsive effort to safely squeeze meaning out of meaninglessness; thus those pathetic carvings on tombstones, thus those expensive funerals with music and obituaries to order. How late and misleading all of that is! If you want to invest in something, then it should be in dying, so we can make it comfortable to the highest possible degree;

because there is, as we can certainly agree, a difference whether someone dunks your head into the stream of shit in London's sewers, or if you're hit in the head, in the pure mountain air, in the middle of sunny luminosity, with a rock disinfected by the primeval effect of natural elements and the last thing you see is the silver sparkle of all the stars right at noon.

They say that cats have nine lives; I have had (and please consider this information confidential) twenty-three so far; this is the twenty-fourth. Because yes, twenty-three times I have already stood on the threshold of death, ten times I have even raised my hand and knocked on the door, but nobody was ever home. Twenty-three times, and each time, regardless of how much the situation took me by surprise, I made sure, within the given range of possibilities, to make, if not the essence, at least the circumstances of my exit to the other world as pleasant as possible. Under the pleasant sense—Pleasant, so to speak, with a capital *P*—I mean that bittersweet feeling that ^{capital *P*} seizes you when they call closing time in a wine bar. Because only the ancient Greeks and the Olympic long-distance champion Nurmi knew how to finish on top, voluntarily, that is.

A bittersweet feeling: sweet with the honey of the present and bitter with the painful realization that it is coming to an end; and honey, as you certainly know, is gathered from the pollen of flowers. I mean all of this symbolically. A country is not a picture of the soul, but it can, at least for a moment, help to raise your self-confidence, to inspire a certain respect, however mistaken, for yourself. . . . When they tried to run me down with a taxi in Bucharest, ^{Bucharest} the two big leaps that I took did not have the goal of snatching myself from the claws of the rapidly oncoming vehicle—it was already too late for that; I just wanted to be able to fall in a place from which I could see the sidewalks of the Boulevard Magheru bordered with trees, beyond the white walls of the Banka de Credit Roman. From a worm's-eye view, it's one of the most beautiful sights ever.

639,789   At the time, Bucharest had 639,789 inhabitants, and if we subtract children and the elderly, there'd be about 300,000 men and women at a productive age, ready at any time to have you run down by a taxi. The charge for that kind of service was quite insignificant. Nowhere could you find more helpful taxi drivers than in Romania. When the national interest required it, King Carol II had the whole government run down by taxis without a moment's hesitation. Today Bucharest has twenty-two theaters, but at the time the favorite form of theater was watching an unfortunate person dodging an attacking taxi in confusion. The popular character of King Carol's rule was proved by the fact that this theater was free of charge. I should mention, only for the sake of comparison, that these days a theater ticket costs 15 lei and an opera ticket as much as 25 lei.

théâtre-vérité   *Théâtre-vérité.* That artistic form is today, and I don't know if entirely rightfully, neglected. . . . Yes, King Carol II was a great patron of the arts; if there was no bread, then there had to be circuses. At the time it had to do, if I'm not mistaken, with the theft of the crown jewels; actually, that theft was forged—who would today, or even then, have stolen the crown jewels, which were practically impossible to sell! King Carol II was insured at Lloyd's of London, and so the theft of the jewels was the easiest way for him to get some cash, and moreover in hard currency. His partners at cards didn't accept anything else. That was already the fifth

6/8/30 time since his accession to the throne—June 8, 1930: what a memory, eh?—and Lloyd's decided firmly that it would be the last: King Carol had to go. Except that, as I have already mentioned, only the ancient Greeks and Nurmi knew how to leave in their prime. Thus I was called by the great Harold Lloyd himself, the one with the horn-rimmed spectacles, and ordered to carry out a dethroning, preserving the monarchy if possible. I did it as an independent contractor.

Have you ever been in the Bucharest train station? One of the dirtiest; but if I can express myself metaphorically, that greasy saucer had a silver border. In Bucharest you could find anything you could get in Paris, and at half the price. In 1933, Romanian imports from Czechoslovakia, for example, were 9.84 percent, and exports to Czechoslo- 9.84% vakia 4.79 percent. Romania mainly exported corn, oil, and live animals. Bessarabian horses were known as the second-best in the world, right after Arabian, and Romania annexed Bessarabia only on December 10, 1918. At the time I'm speaking of, Japan had still not ratified that annexation. As you can see from the small amount of data I've given you, the international situation was quite complicated at the moment I got off in front of the Splendid-Parc Hotel Splendid-Parc on Strada Știrbei Voda, right across from the king's palace.

It was a hotel favored by diplomats, industrialists, and representatives of the business world. I personally decided on the role of an English financier, primarily for the reason that the greater part of my luggage was in the form of a gentleman's large umbrella.

Are you in a hurry? I wanted to dwell on that umbrella for a moment. It was a made-to-order specimen, not like today's assembly-line merchandise, constructed of cheap material that gets porous when it dries and then lets the rain through. The top was fashioned out of bulletproof steel covered with camouflaged canvas, so that when opened, it represented a perfect shield, and even a hiding place (especially on the battlefield). At the same time, the hilt was the handle for a concealed pistol; in the middle was a hollow safe with a password, and at the end a bayonet which sprang out at the push of a spring. It was a superb umbrella, but they stole it from me right at the reception desk. If we take into consid- reception desk eration that Bucharest was a favorite center for pickpockets, one didn't even know whether to suspect bad intentions.

The great number of successfully resolved cases could have lulled me into a falsely carefree mood, but the incident with the umbrella served as an early warning. Because even if it had been an unknown thief without bad intentions and the theft was just a routine matter, surely such an suspicious umbrella must have seemed suspicious upon closer inspection. The spring had a little problem—the bayonet would pop out at the most unexpected moments. When opening the top, it sometimes happened that one would unknowingly press the cock in the handle and the umbrella fired accidentally. Although I had long since removed the label with the name of the manufacturer, so the umbrella could preserve its complete incognito, its versatility could not stay concealed for long. More than one adventure could be waiting for me, thanks to that umbrella—whether during the harvest festival or some other entirely inconvenient occasion. Therefore I decided that before proceeding to the matter at hand, I would start off with some warming-up exercises for my fingers, by searching out the umbrella's misappropriator and making him pay for his mischief.

Romanian hotel suites! I mean, Romanian chamber-2 little snakes maids! With hands as skillful as two little snakes, she had made up my bed for the night and in order to demonstrate its total safety and comfort to me, a distrustful foreigner, she lay down on it with sensuous delight. Well, perhaps while opening my suitcase I had somehow pushed her a little. From the position her body had instinctively taken in its fall, I concluded that these surroundings were not entirely unknown to her. I was also able to glimpse that under the simple black dress with the little white collar, there was Jaeger nothing except Jaeger's-brand woolen underwear; but I didn't manage to determine whether that part of her clothing was her only memento of her prematurely deceased father, or whether it was a feminine variant of the popular underwear widespread in Romania.

As it turned out, there I committed another error. From the point of view of my already-considerable renown, it was naturally better that I committed these errors in remote

Romania, and not in the center of world attention, somewhere in Paris or London. From the point of view of my
personal safety, however, this difference was completely
negligible. If I had paid less attention to the smooth velvet
of her body and more to the underwear which she discreetly lowered beside the bed, I would have noticed that
the hem of the underwear was marked with an inventory
number and the words INSURED WITH LLOYD'S. By my
proverbial sharpness I would not have later failed to realize . . . are you following me?

I can perceive a certain resentment in your face, coming from the fact that I have not devoted my exclusive
attention to the details of the physical intercourse. I warn
you in advance that I am an opponent of eroticism for its
own sake. I don't deny, naturally, the role that sexuality   sexuality
plays in human life; if it weren't for sexuality, what would
really separate us from the animals? But, for God's sake,
women! Moist, as the decadent French writer Simone de
Beauvoir admitted self-critically, in the middle! But a person in a foreign country needs to create a certain base. . . .

Kissing, for example, has been observed in chimpanzees.
But also female flat-footed baboons from the New World—
Alouatta pallida—often, during mating, turn and move at   *Alouatta*
the same time with the tongue toward the male and often   *pallida*
lick him. Elephants also "kiss" in an interesting manner
before mating, with the ends of their trunks in each other's
mouths. One native of the Thonga tribe in Mozambique
commented symptomatically on the European kiss with the
words: "Those two are drinking each other's saliva!"

But why waste all these words? The mating of many
mammals does not look like an act of love, but like a strug-   act of love
gle, in which the female first tries to run away, then to fight,
and retaliates with a hit although, in view of her physical disposition, she finally has to lose. At the end of their decade of
sexual activity, the females of various apes are covered with
the scars that come from amorous relations. I'd rather not

even mention the males. Do you want to have a look? In his studies of the sexual lives of Pacific tribes, Malinowski discovered that women employ much more passionate and painful practices of sexual games and coitus. I, who was more practically than theoretically engaged in the field referred to, can confirm his observations on the basis of my own experience. In particular, Romanian chambermaids . . . but admit it, you have a premonition that she wasn't a chambermaid at all. What did you say? You don't have any premonitions? Don't deprive me of my last illusions. So she simply wasn't a real chambermaid. You say that this isn't essential in intercourse? My dear friend, don't let it show so obviously that you are swayed by the opinions of your generation. You have, I must regretfully state, inverted values. Intercourse in and of itself is not substantial, especially when, as in this case, it's only business intercourse.

Of course, I didn't mean to say that we took care of this only standing on one leg. It's necessary to give the body what it deserves. It is, if I could speak openly, as if you would suck your thumb. To wit . . . in the case at hand it 4 phases was different—we experienced all four phases of male and female sexual activity. To tell you the truth, we passed through the phase of stimulation more or less at a trot. Experienced individuals can allow themselves to do that. On the other hand, we stayed longer in the plateau phase. Looking over her shoulder, I tried to penetrate deeper into the mystery of the Jaeger woolen underwear, while she for her part tried to penetrate deeper into the back pocket of my trousers—where I had, however, circumspectly only hidden my unpaid receipts from the dry cleaner's. Although this fact didn't need to be made public, I didn't consider it useful, on the other hand, to conceal it at all costs: I had soiled eight shirts and twelve pairs of under- month of April wear in the month of April. I admit that in the back of my mind, I hoped that if she saw the amount of the required sum, she would offer to do my laundry herself during my stay in Romania. Therefore, I didn't particularly insist on crossing over as soon as possible to the phase of relaxation, either.

Right when I was able to figure out the inventory number on the backside of the Jaeger underwear, the dear chambermaid, who was really no chambermaid at all, reached orgasm. That was something! If the whole thing had taken place after ten o'clock at night, they certainly would have thrown us out for disturbing the peace. I was willing to tolerate that she bit my throat, but when she dug four bloody furrows with her nails into my cheek, it aroused in me the suspicion—unfortunately, as it turned out, a justified one—that she intentionally wanted to leave a mark on me.

Women, as is well known, know how to simulate orgasm, but an experienced man of my stature (at the time I measured one meter, eighty-four centimeters) can't be fooled so easily; in such situations, young man, I watch the woman's nipples: initiates know that if a woman reaches orgasm, her nipples wrinkle up immediately after intercourse; otherwise this process takes longer. 1.84 m

So I watched, and what should I tell you. That pseudo-chambermaid was the greatest European actress after the immortal Eleanora Duse. She lay there blushing, with her wrinkled-up nipples, and when she noticed my penetrating look, she turned up her palms and chattered in charming Romanian: "*Csak egy kis emlék,* a little souvenir from you...." I couldn't get angry with her, although during the first orgasmic spasm she had skillfully knocked my suitcase off the bed, so that its entire contents landed on the carpet, spread out like goods on a vegetable stand. I have to say that in my contacts with the colonel, whatever reservations one may have about them, such awkward intermezzos did not take place.... When the colonel's head dropped down to the soft little hollow above my collarbone, no suitcase was knocked over. Why? you might ask. It certainly wasn't just because there was no suitcase there. Even at his peak of Eleanora Duse

intermezzo

EVER GREEN IS . . .

49

manly power, the colonel's movements retained a genuine tenderness and graciousness—there is ultimately nothing better than a demonstration; let me see . . . you have, dear friend, a completely cozy little hollow. It reminds me of my eventful youth. Well, when the colonel's head lowered down, it wasn't like a falling rock; it was a light landing, as when a bird arrives at her nest, bringing food for her young; like a little feather, which was left floating behind, forgotten in the air. . . .

Couldn't you take off your shirt? Because when I see for myself, I can empathize better. What, I should use my rich imagination instead? Dear friend, according to the Freud Viennese Jew Freud, the creator of psychoanalysis, a happy person doesn't have fantasies, only a person who is unfulfilled in life has them. And that, I believe, cannot be said of me. It's true, one can realize, that psychoanalysis as a movement, as a certain doctrine, arose in certain socioeconomic conditions and was based on certain theoretical assumptions, also important from a conceptual viewpoint, that carry particular weight in the current ideological conflict of two world systems.

Don't worry, you won't catch a cold, I'll close the window. What? Give the body what it deserves, and give the soul . . . in your case, I don't dare to speak of the soul. Mandatory school attendance sometimes causes more damage than benefit. You had too many old-maid schoolteachers. Shouldn't Aristotle I turn on the record player? Aristotle saw the advantage of music in releasing passions. An igniting of passion in drama is also a good thing. Such an occasional igniting of passion gives people some relief. And no one needs relief as urgently as one of us, who live in constant tension. A demonstration of this, if I may cite the first example that comes to mind, was the expression of immense relief on the face of the Romanian anti-chambermaid when she observed that the suitcase did not contain an automatic pistol. A relief so limitless that I considered it a warning at the moment. But before I had a chance to follow that thought through to the end—I was extraordinarily clever, but in certain situations I wasn't able to concentrate—she groped for my head with her hands, and as if by chance, she suddenly covered my ears with her palms. To prevent me from hearing the turn of the door-knob, she pulled me down to her breasts. From this you can see that when taking action, you shouldn't follow thoughts, but people.

I lay in the warm valley between her breasts for only a second, and already I had realized the acute danger in which I had found myself: her heart was beating unusually fast. At least, I would estimate now, something like 140 beats a minute. I didn't really have time then for a precise calculation; with just one mighty leap, I threw myself at the table lamp and . . . 140/min.

6

Oh, sweet shivers of danger! Oh, its edge, put to my throat! Bow of highest tones! The little singing poison-toothed reed! On the other hand, sweet! Cool to the touch! Antenna of the beyond! In moments of danger I believe in the other world; it's really only a kind of mnemotechnical aid . . . a pebble thrown at the window of the universe, behind which the intoxicatingly golden-haired Sleeping Beauty was dreaming! A longing written with a finger on a misted-up window! Wiped with one's own breath! It would go more easily, naturally, by hand, but that would contradict the character of danger—which, as you certainly know, cuts the ropes of the anchors of reality with the cries of seagulls. And the sails of human will are already swelling, the proud prow is already towering above the waves. . . . Sleeping Beauty

If this doesn't interest you, you can go for a walk, but don't yawn so provocatively. I love danger; in our line of work it can't be any other way, and once I start talking about it . . . danger, the footman of death—yet the faithful servant the footman of death of life! The torch of excitement illuminates its noble features. Well, this stylization will certainly need more thought. Are you creative? The torments of creativity, stretched on the rack of an ideal, tied up in its tail, and the ideal, that exuberant magical stallion . . . I'm speaking generally, because your stallion, as far as I can see, is just an ordinary carcass.

Well, fine, let's skip that. In our line of work, and I'm saying this as friendly advice, one cannot do without an ideal. And without a love, a sincere, unconditional love of danger. Danger—the Polaris of our vigilant nights! The flint that strikes the spark! Unquenchable thirst! Now try it yourself. Yes, boldly! Danger—the mother of wisdom? Don't delude yourself—its pregnancy often ends in a miscarriage. If anything, then danger—the whip of inspiration. But you haven't really matured enough for this yet. Try something easier. . . .

You give up? You don't have a competitive spirit. I have a feeling you don't distinguish between reality and life. Yes, reality is often hard, implacable, and pays us little attention; but life is violent, harsh, swift-flowing; a tale of which we are the storytellers. . . . Reality, however cruel, however dejected, is only one aspect of life. If we discover obstacles on the way to our goal that cannot be avoided, we should overcome them with a frontal blow, that is, direct remove or smash through them, that is to say, with direct aggression. A drop of water carves out a stone not with force, but because it keeps dripping. It is true, in civilized countries, aggressive behavior that threatens other people, and many times the interests of society, is evaluated predominantly negatively and punished. But this mustn't scare our people. I decidedly refuse the various elite theories, but on the other hand, in the interest of preserving the ability to act, we must know how to turn a blind eye on ourselves, even both eyes if necessary.

For example, to progress from the known to the unknown, it is certainly not proper to break lamps in hotels favored by diplomats, industrialists, and representatives of the business world. But a person who would, in the given situation, let his hands be tied by social considerations and formalities, would be hopelessly lost. Not me. They soon found me, lying under the bed, where I had cleverly managed to roll under cover of darkness.

There are situations in which even the most talented people should know when to admit defeat. For example, admitting it is said that a wolf, when a fight is turning out extremely defeat unfavorably for him, will suddenly expose to his opponent his most vulnerable place—his throat. The reaction of the opponent to this signal is to interrupt the fight. So it was in our case. Creeping out from under the bed to confront my opponents—to speak concretely, there were two of them—I exposed not my throat, since I am ultimately not a wolf, but rather my private parts, in all their naked beauty. I noticed a gleam of open admiration flash in their eyes at this imposing sight. But they were professionals professionals and nothing could distract them from the task entrusted to them.

I forgot to mention that thanks to my skillful, if somewhat delayed, manipulation of the lamp, my opponent's first blow did not strike me, but the unlucky pseudochambermaid, who was now lying unconscious on the bed just as the Lord had created her, and I must add objectively that he did a good job. After all, I was not among the rejects, either. Still, today, at the end of a long and difficult rejects life. . . . Don't worry, I'm only unbuttoning this because it's getting hot in here.

Yet the two hired bullies were made like tools: for a single purpose. They fulfilled it when they firmly tied up my arms and legs and rolled me up in a carpet—I should mention, it was not out of innate modesty, but so that they wouldn't attract undue attention out in the hallway. Then they took up reviving their collaborator. They were not suited for that purpose. It took them rather long to realize that, and during that time, I finally figured out the writing on the backside of the Jaeger long johns, which were lying on the floor right next to my head. And when I read the fateful words INSURED WITH LLOYD'S, I understood why I had not received any foreign postcards for so long from my friend Seppi Wodopiwczo, a detective with the firm of Anglo-Danubian Lloyd, Allgemeine Versicherungs-Aktien-Gesellschaft, headquartered in Vienna I, Dominikaner-bastei 2. This knowledge would have paralyzed more than one man in my situation—I was a serious collector of post-cards, and it was clear that one of my main sources had dried up for good—but I, a lover of danger . . . the bigger, the better . . .

Anglo-Danubian

Danger is like a woman: it should have a certain volume. So that (if I may be vulgar) there's something to grab on to. There are actually matadors who grab on to danger like a bull by the horns, but those are ordinary hired hands, who do a trade for wages, without love. But artists— among whom I (with all modesty) count myself—know that danger should be fondled, tickled, caressed, patted on its chubby little bottom. Dangers, and I mean the real ones, usually have little roundish bottoms, as perhaps you've noticed, with a little cleavage . . . roundish and bouncing. When they rub against each other in such a neighborly way with both hemispheres, it's as if a solar reflection jumped from one window to another; while the others drag their asses, as if pouring sour milk from one bottle to another. Such backsides, along with the dangers that belong to them, are passé, a millstone tied around your neck. No doubt those kinds of dangers don't have great demands, but if you strike up a conversation with them, you'll never be able to shake them off. They aren't even real dangers, and an experienced observer recognizes them by the backside; they're just ordinary fears: for example, that you displease your boss because you forget to turn off the light in the restroom. . . .

matadors

sour milk

EVER GREEN IS . . .

Ugh! Pour some more; let me get rid of that aftertaste. Ugh!
Now, where were we? Ah yes, in the Splendid-Parc Hotel,
rolled up in a carpet. "Dear Colonel," I said then, naturally only in my mind, since my mouth was gagged with a
handkerchief—from the taste I concluded that its owner
was suffering from a chronic cold; just a detail, you say,
but a person never knows when it might come in handy
—"Dear Colonel," I said then, "what would you do in
my place?"

"Dear friend," replied the colonel, "I answer you along
with Confucius: If you can't defend yourself against rape, Confucius
you should lie back and enjoy it."

Nothing else was left for me to do but to repeat those
words again. A person who knows how to enjoy life in all
its forms may not ultimately live longer, but certainly lives
more intensely. Do you know how much I enjoyed it when
they unrolled me from the stuffy atmosphere inside the
carpet, into the cool darkness of a cell inside a royal castle?
And my enjoyment grew even more (if that were possible
at all) when they seated me, naked as I was, astride a long
pole made of ice, hung on two hooks above a spacious
iron tub, filled to the brim with sulfuric acid. The only sulfuric acid
thing that dampened my pleasure was the fear of catching
diaper rash. This fear was, as many fears have been, exaggerated: in view of the minimal thickness of the ice I
could have caught, at most, a teeny little rash; in the
meantime the ice would have melted from my body heat
—my anus, which was actually at stake, so to speak, was
37 degrees Celsius at that moment—and I would have 37° C
fallen, tied at hand and foot, with no resistance, into the
tub of acid. Informally, they called this primitive-looking
but effective arrangement the "accelerator."

Here I should mention that the equipment of the cell
was in sharp contrast to the scientific requirements a
similar place would be subject to today. In any kind of
workplace, there should be an interior setting, or climate, climate

which optimally suits the human organism. I don't mean to say, naturally, that the cold of the old walls was unpleasant in the first few moments, but later, not very comfortably seated on the ice. . . . The folk wisdom in the proverbial "to put something on ice" long ago grasped that it had to do with an experience which was essentially negative. One understandably does not expect that he'll be handled with kid gloves, but still . . .

An interrogation room should be suitably equipped, culturally speaking. But since it is not possible to assume that all arrivals are accustomed to a similar culture of interiors, whether from their domestic setting or workplace —rather the opposite, especially among recidivists, alcoholics and such people—it is not possible to neglect the gradual necessity for the gradual adaptation of a new arrival to an adaptation interrogation room. That was out of the question in my case. So you can understand my exasperation when I had to watch how they broke the basic rules of interrogating practice before my very eyes. Everyone who has dealt even superficially with this problem knows that the change from one setting to another cannot be sudden, but must be interior a gradual adaptation. The interior shouldn't be so showy— by the way, some pelvis bones and skulls were scattered in the corner of the cell, so at first glance it was clear that it hadn't been tidied up in a while—rather, it should meet the demands of the times. Some sectional furniture, both in the waiting room and in the investigator's office, would have been appropriate. And not some pole of ice, which is, *nota bene,* thoroughly unadapted to the bodily dimensions of the person being interrogated!

I tell you frankly, one glance at that uncultured, unhy-
British gienic room was enough to know that my British passport
passport —a false one, by the way—wouldn't be worth a thing. It was not possible to characterize the role of the interrogators as other than biased, although as a rule, an interrogator should form a relationship to the person he is interrogating only on

the basis of objective knowledge, and even then, he should suppress it as much as possible. You might say that it's a waste of energy to painstakingly establish a relationship which we need to immediately suppress as much as possible, this seemingly senseless activity is really useful for venting surplus energy and distracts the interrogator from excessive concentration on the interrogated subject's personality.

In this case, however, the desired dispersion of attention did not occur. As soon as they seated me (not especially comfortably) on the ice, the first stupid question they immediately asked was: "Who are you and who sent you?" Karneyeva et al. claim, it is true, that the classifications of Tarasov-Rodionov, Feygin, and other authors concerning the differentiation of questions into various types have a purely relative meaning, but I remain of the opinion that it was a stupid question. I don't have in mind the error made frequently by interrogators, namely that the questions they ask are suggestive, and for people with a higher level of suggestibility, such as children, oligophrenics, paranoid people, hysterics, and the senile demented, they actually determine the character of the answer in advance; such questions are, on the contrary, an outright pleasure for the interrogatee, who readily meets the interrogators' expectations halfway. For example, when the Kellogg couple asked their chimpanzee, "Do you want some orange?" it responded with an affirmative, agreeing sound. The general rule applies that one needs to agree with the interrogators as much as possible. Now we know that suggestion does not penetrate into the psyche through the main entrance, by way of logical persuasion, but through the back entrance; we could say by avoiding the "ego," the personal consciousness and will. It is—and now I am again speaking on the basis of my own rich experience—it is meaningless to call on an interrogator's common sense and explain to him that we have no idea about the whole thing. He won't believe you, and that's as it should be. On

Karneyeva et al.

paranoid people

suggestion

the basis of this assumption, you can tell the truth here and there, if nothing better occurs to you.

As the basic rule has it: To a suggestive question, give a suggestive answer. Raise interest with a decoration, with an ornament; emphasize the form and suppress the content.

who discovered America

So to the question "Who discovered America?" an experienced interrogatee will answer, "I'd swear on my life that it was Christopher Columbus," or "In view of well-known circumstances, it is possible to assume that it was Christopher Columbus." Eighty out of a hundred interrogators would soon ask: "So you'd swear on your life? Were you there?" or "What well-known circumstances are you alluding to?" The more arrogant ones, and it is well known that one interrogator is more arrogant than the next, will not resist biting remarks like: "Who cares about your life here?" or "You seem to know an awful lot about those circumstances. . . ." One way or the other, the direction of the interrogation has shifted and it has long been forgotten that America was discovered by the Viking seafarer Erik the Red.

Binet and Stern

Of course, not all questions are alike. A. Binet and W. Stern have divided suggestive questions into several groups according to the power of their suggestive influence. While Stern, for example, distinguishes six groups, Lipmann comes up with as many as eight. First, reporting questions; for example: "What do you want?" Let's assume, just so we can stay in familiar territory, that the answer is: "An orange." Second are the questions that require qualification, that begin with the words who, what, when, where:

what kind of orange?

"What kind of orange?" Third, generally alternative questions, that is, those that take into consideration all of the possibilities: "Do you want the orange with the peel, without the peel, or are you going to eat the peel and the pulp separately?" Personally, for example, I dry the peel and dip it in sugar. Fourth, decisive questions; for example: "Was it raining when you felt like having an orange?"

Fifth, affirmative determining questions; for example: "Does an orange have a thick peel?" Sixth . . . were you able to write that part down? Sixth, determining and denying questions; for example: "Doesn't an orange have a thick peel?" Seventh, completely separative questions; for example: "Does an orange have a thick peel, or is it without a peel?" And we have already, as you see, separated the orange from the peel. Eighth and last, questions counting on mistaken assumptions; for example: "Would you eat an orange if you weren't afraid that it would oxidize your dentures?" Well, would you? Answer if someone asks you nicely.

You mean you don't have dentures? That's nothing; it's easily taken care of. You haven't understood anything. A symptom always conceals more than it reveals. Where is my tidbit, the plush bunny that my greyhound of imagination would run after? Every interrogation is a certain form of compromise, and a compromise cannot be made with empty hands. An offer! Those who have nothing else will ultimately offer a complete confession. The self-confidence of neurotics is always on shaky ground. Such a compromise is unacceptable; it is not even a compromise, but an absolute surrender. Equally unacceptable is the situation when instead of the trivial facts that the interrogator mostly already knows, the interrogatee puts his own physical health, or even his life, on the scale, and perishes with a closed mouth. Mark my words, that is not heroism, but helplessness.

The basic rule of a person who enters the form of human communication known as interrogation in the role of the interrogatee is that the interrogator must get his own. He has to be entertained, amused, and emotionally satisfied, as well as enriching his knowledge. There are even individuals (whom I would call geniuses of interrogation) who manage to educate the interrogator in the course of an interrogation. By "educate" in this concrete case, I mean accentuating the positive human qualities and suppressing the negative ones.

symptom

scale

educate

Of course, genius is really the highest and most socially productive form of mental defect. As the notable German psychiatrist Ernst Kretschmer correctly writes in his interesting monograph about geniuses, psychopathy per se is quite certainly not an entry pass to Parnassus. Quite certainly not, dear Kretschmer, I say myself, on the basis of my own experience too; but why imagine Parnassus as

dormitory some kind of girls' dormitory? Who cares about your Parnassus, dear Kretschmer? An entry pass! The real genius of a genius is that he weaves his own unrepeatable Parnassus from his own body like a spiderweb! We are, dear Kretschmer, our own Parnassi, and we enthrone ourselves on mountaintops even without your entry passes! In Nepal, they give passes to mountain climbers who are get-

Mt. Everest ting ready to go up Mount Everest, but in the realm of the spirit . . . but that, dear Kretschmer, you cannot understand.

What's that? I know, my dear friend, that your name is not Kretschmer. I'm foaming at the mouth? That's ordinary saliva; I can dry it off like this with my sleeve. A cigarette? Give me two, and remember for the future that conventional offers of cigarettes, like "Light up, you'll feel better, calm down," and that kind of thing are cheap, tactless forms of behavior, more suitable for a failed staging of a detective story. Such a schematic approach is, in its effect, in contrast with understanding the individuality of a person as a unique individual. But this, dear Kretschmer, you cannot comprehend.

7

Who are you and who sent you? Don't be frightened, dear friend; I'm not asking you—that was the question put to me by my torturers under the vaulted ceiling of the royal dungeon. Did I say torturers? Then I wronged them, or at least I forestalled the following events, because when that question was asked, I was sitting, if not comfortably then at least completely undisturbed, on my icy throne. On the other hand, I cannot help admitting that my experiences up to that point gave me a certain right to use that word; it wasn't the first time I had found myself in a situation like that and I was able to foresee with near certainty, even (as they say in our circles) to directly anticipate the things to come.

Imagine that you're going to see your dentist. We can use this entirely ordinary but unpleasant event to divide people into two basic types: suicidal and avoiding. Suicidal people are those determined individuals who repeatedly knock on the door of the dentist's office, demanding entrance, then when they're taken in, they refuse an injection and urge the dentist that they just want to have the whole thing over with as soon as possible. The avoiding type include hesitaters, who find out on the way to the dentist that their teeth have stopped hurting and try to persuade themselves that this accidental and mostly untrue circumstance means a change in the progress of the disease; if they finally do reach the waiting room, they infallibly find out that it's too crowded and that their turn wouldn't come anyway that day; sometimes they even run down the back staircase with their jaws as hard as a stone from pain-killing shots; and even in the dentist's chair, they persuade the dentist with their mouths wide open that he's probably quite tired after a long day's work and that they would gladly come some other time. Have you ever had your teeth extracted? You still have all of them? You're an amateur, or greenhorn, as they say—which isn't, I might add, the same as a blues trumpet.

Well, let's drop it. It's enough to say that the position of people waiting for torture is in essence similar. You can tell a professional, that is to say a professional martyr, because he doesn't succumb to his instinctive inclinations, but he carefully conceives a mental scenario of his own torture. This art, one of the most difficult, can only be taught to you by life itself. That is, of course, if you have a

anticipate

2 types

greenhorn

disposition for it (to avoid using the currently rather over-
talent used word "talent").

So when the question was asked "Who are you and who
sent you?" I answered without hesitation, "Dear Colonel
Alfredl, I am your admirer, and I was not sent, but driven
here by the sincere feeling that flared up quite unexpectedly in my heart."

When the colonel asked the above-mentioned question,
his lips were sinking into the charming (I say "charming"
because there are moments when a false modesty must
take second place to an objective judgment) little hollow
above my collarbone. I could have pretended I didn't quite
understand him, to win some precious time; but I realized
that if I won some time, precious as it may have been, I
would lose the colonel's trust, and that was much more
precious for me. I did not have the slightest doubt that
such an all-powerful man as the colonel had everything at
his disposal to have verified all of my personal data long
ago, and this seemingly important conversation would serve
only as a pretext to penetrate deeper and deeper into the
thicket thicket of physical passions. His effort, however, was not
of physical in direct contrast with my own goal, so acting nonchalant
passions and as if unaware, focusing on the questions, I unbuttoned
some of the buttons on my trousers.

Blinded with his own desire, the colonel mistakenly
took the reflection of the red walls on my face for a virginal
blush and gave himself up to his sexual urges. I don't know
how it was generally—that is, I couldn't allow myself such
luxury a luxury—but in that concrete case his urges, in contrast to
a stream of water, which has more of a tendency to horizon-
tal movement, started in a vertical direction. He staggered
and fell to the floor, and with him also fell my trousers, to
which he was convulsively holding on.

I was not an expert, but even my superficial health
training was enough for me to know that before my eyes
grand mal was occurring a grand mal, that is, as a certain nation in

the heart of Europe better known for beer than bravery might say, a big cock-up. In other words, a big screw-up. Someone else in my place—you, for example (although, frankly speaking, I can't imagine that even in my wildest fantasies)—would have made use of the situation, and, relying on the fact that the colonel was not going to remember anything after his seizure, would have stuffed his pockets with a few valuable objects and tiptoed away. But I was not so shortsighted, and at that moment I was thinking not of momentary gain, but of my future.

A person who in stressful moments does not hold his future tightly in his hands can never determine the future of the masses. And to me, if you want to hear my own personal declaration, it had to do with nothing less. So I stepped out of the trousers, which the colonel was still convulsively clutching in his hands, and stepped into history. *stepping into* Sitting on the Empire settee, which was tenderly stroking *history* my naked thighs, I gave myself up . . . not to the colonel— you're licking your lips in vain—nor to the nonexistent mistress of the house, but to feverish consideration, because I had fully realized—everything that I've done in life, I've done fully—that if I could find out what had caused the colonel's sudden seizure, I would gain a powerful weapon that I would be able to use frequently in the future.

As is well known, the direct causes of epileptic seizures may vary. One Russian composer (who was treated by the famous Russian neurologist Bekhterev) had seizures when listening to a certain aria from the opera *The Snow Maiden,* *Snow Maiden* even when the aria was sung very well. The most common visual stimulus is a blinking light that varies in intensity. There is also a well-known theory according to which a seizure indicates a surplus of fluids in the body.

I thought over one cause after another. The only acoustic stimulus that I could remember was the sound of buttons being unbuttoned, but this was more imagined than real and could not provoke such a violent response. As for visual

stimuli, those were also essentially poor—not that my
almost naked body wouldn't have been a visual tidbit even
for the most refined gourmet, which the colonel undoubtedly was, but because right at the beginning of our caresses,
I had, from youthful shyness and, why hide it, also slyness,
switched off the lamp. It had a pink lace lampshade—I can
see it as if it were yesterday. At that moment—now that
I have come all the way here in my thoughts . . . don't look
at my finger, I don't mean here, I mean there—at that
moment, I switched the lamp on again.

The light bulb, as is the custom in more intimate apart-
ments, was not very strong, but it did not escape my attention that the colonel's eyelids had slightly trembled. They
had trembled like the fiber of a spiderweb in the breeze of a
moth's wings. They had trembled like the gentlest little hair,
for which even a shiver was like an earthquake tremor. They
had trembled . . . try it yourself. I know that you weren't
there. They were trembling like the ninth featherbed of the
spoiled princess when a pea rolled under her mattress. But
they were trembling, and that microscopic movement did
not escape my sharp eye.

This doesn't document anything but a certain percep-
tiveness; the important thing is what you do with a fact
discovered in this way. You, for example, so that we may
speak concretely, you would have succumbed to the first
impulse—if we disregard the most probable eventuality
that you would have marched right down the stairs at that
moment and with hands damp from excitement, would
have hidden the colonel's silver letter opener (whose handle would have been, *nota bene,* decorated with an aristo-
cratic crown and the colonel's initials, so that it would have
been worthless from a financial viewpoint and it could have
served only as a corpus delicti or as a souvenir). Quiet, I'm
speaking now. You, my dear stupid friend, certainly would
have called out immediately: "Don't play cat and mouse with
me, Colonel!" or (but this is pure flattery) you would have

blurted out more wittily, though still unwisely: "I'm glad, dear Colonel, that this seizure of yours has already passed."

Not me. That's what makes the real difference in our styles—I accepted this no doubt important fact as it was intended: as a secret. With lightning speed, which, however, does not mean hasty consideration, I reached the conclusion that it was not necessary and not even desirable to astound the colonel with my thorough medical knowledge, so I left in feigned embarrassment and uncertainty to find the bathroom. medical knowledge

I don't need to emphasize—but in your case I think it may do no harm—that I used this opportunity to become thoroughly familiar with the colonel's apartment. After a carefully measured moment, I returned with a glass of water and a wet towel; I put the first to the colonel's mouth, the second to his heart. As I had assumed, the colonel used the offered opportunity to return honorably among the conscious, and when some cold water trickled down his chin onto his neck, he groaned several times and opened his eyes.

As groans go, these ones were not particularly convincing . . . between the second and third he even burped . . . but have you ever opened your eyes after passing out completely? At that moment when you realize this world is only a little splinter of the universe? When your pupils are still dilated with a reflection of superreality? No, let's try it another way: Have you seen, have you ever witnessed, a woman opening her eyes after successfully completing intercourse? splinter of the universe

Oh, of course. How silly of me to ask. Excuse me. Don't be upset about that; what is not can still be. Although, when I have a better look at you, not necessarily. How old are you? There are well-known cases when an adolescent, after a certain groping, is able to master coitus without previous instruction. Nevertheless, it just seems that these instincts are more weakly developed in humans than in the lower mammals, which succeed in the first attempt at coitus. Naturally, I don't want to intrude on your private life . . . don't first attempt blush; it doesn't become you anymore . . . but tell me, have you ever tried it? I don't need to ask about the result. After all, the important thing is that a maturing youth is satisfied with everything, even with an imperfect sexual encounter, and learns gradually. On the other hand, a late-starting intellectual—but this won't be your case—is often psychically shattered in the course of a first unsuccessful attempt at coitus. The oversensitivity of today's men has acquired ominous dimensions.

If you don't know any other way to hide your embarrassment, pour me some more. And don't droop your head, when your other parts are already drooping. We observe a sexual cooling-off now and then also at such times when a man must restrict fatty and rich foods—for example, on a diet for diseases of the liver, stomach, or kidneys. You say you're physically healthy? Remember that overly sensitive people, who easily start whining, quickly get worn out by life and later are unable to experience sexual life joyfully. Although who cares about joy . . . have you ever been a thumb-sucker? I don't mean sucking your own thumb. Sucking your thumb in childhood is an unmistakable symptom of emotional frustration.

The man who enjoys his sexual life most fully is the one who is able to experience it uninterruptedly with his whole being. When I say uninterruptedly, I don't mean bolting the doors with two locks, so that you're not interrupted penetration when your parents come home. Penetration as an introduction to copulation is the last state of aggression. A drop erodes a rock not in that way, but differently. In cases when emotional interest . . . the single interest of which you are capable . . . impedes on real closeness, it is no surprise that your attempts at copulation fail. Individuals can lie to each other during contractation, but it's harder during amplectation, which therefore lacks adequate accentation. As the proverb says, without appetite you'll just eat a little bit of shit. Although, when there's nothing else. . . .

A person who wants to knead the soil of history with soil of history his own hands . . . dirty work, I tell you; not for your delicate little white hands . . . do you go to a manicurist? You must; every self-respecting lady spy earns extra income as a manicurist, or is it the other way around? Every time I came to a new, unfamiliar town, I always jumped into the public baths right away . . . it's like when an ambassador delivers his credentials. Of course, you shouldn't ask for the best, but for the most beautiful masseuse.

Don't expect too much from life. Just a few pleasant moments . . . have you been to a First Communion? Long decorative candles, dark blue trousers—navy blue, naturally—as deep as the view into the bottom of an abyss . . . no, maybe a little, but only slightly more shallow; like, let's say, the view into the bottom of a glass. Did you come up with your favorite color yet? So pick one quickly; I think that burnt sienna is momentarily free.

Life, although short, puts us through many tests. Only those who are most resistant, who don't lose heart. . . . Sometimes coitus awakens female reactivity, which is only female reactivity exhausted after several sessions of intercourse or orgasms. And if it doesn't get exhausted, then you do. Avoid cheap thrills. Ejaculation can take place without a sufficient erection during convulsive laughing or throttling. Do you want to try it? Likewise, schoolboys and high school students say that during anxious excitement, for example, during written exams in difficult subjects, they sometimes experience an ejaculation without local stimulation and often even without a sufficient erection, purely out of fear that they won't finish the task in time. It's happened to you before, hasn't it? In my case, if I have to reach into my own memories, I got a terrific erection at the question that was put to me by my teachers, I mean, torturers: "Who are you, who are you? and where did you come from?" Well, if I have to quote precisely, the question went: "Who are you, where did you come from, and where are you going?"

"Whew!" I replied, and in the pause that I fell into after that sigh, my member curiously, or I would even say threateningly, raised its head, which is *glans* in Latin. . . . Do you *sine ira* know Latin? And how could you? *Sine ira et studio.* . . .

I myself looked at that exclamation mark with a poorly concealed envy; that is, it's hard to conceal anything on a naked body. If I were to express myself objectively, there was something provocative in that look—a kind of inappropriate willfulness, I would say. In short, a lurking suspicion overtook me, if there was anything for it to overtake, because I was almost entirely in the power of the king's executioner.

"Whew!" I sighed then again, and the best witness to the quality of my erection was the fact that although this sigh came from the very bottom of my troubled heart, the erect member did not even tremble. "Whew!" I have asked myself that question in moments of peaceful contemplation and to this day I haven't been able to answer it in a satisfactory way. Thus it would have been highly improvident to assume. . . .

shut up! "Shut up!" answered the big lugs, and with eyes widened in amazement, they watched the proudly towering proof of my manhood in disbelief.

"When I came," I said hastily, in an effort to save the situation (in my place, you would have tried to save yourself, but I, pure in my unselfishness, put myself in the last place even at that moment), "I listened to the yearning in my heart—it was my heart, and nothing else, that led me straight to your beautiful city, which is very fittingly called the Paris of the East. But if I were to be frank—and I think London that's what you expect of me—the name London of the South would be similarly appropriate."

See, there you have a classic, high-quality, suggestive answer! To a question which, I must admit, was relatively symptomless. In the end, it was only meant to subtly suggest that I was a supporter of the pedestrian movement. In view of the condition of the railway network in Romania at

the time—11,206 kilometers, but the state they were in!— 11,206 km
it was a completely justified presumption.

London of the South, now come on! But, as I had anticipated, the comparison aroused their interest. It unobtrusively, discreetly flattered them. London of the South! So
then one could, I read it in their faces, just as well call London the Bucharest of the North! The man who was leading the interrogation—his cheeks were furrowed with
deep scars; razor blades as we know them were practically
an unknown concept in Romania at the time—accepted
the flattery with a badly concealed smile, but unlike the
others, he didn't let it lead him away from the basic idea
of interrogation.

Like other artistic forms, interrogation has its own basic
idea, which we must strictly differentiate from its theme.
Themes can be and have been various, but the basic idea
is the same in most interrogations: it is a celebration of man. celebration
"Lo and behold," a successful interrogation seems to relate, of man
"what a man can achieve with a little time and a couple of
simple instruments!" Today's complex equipment is only,
believe me, a concession to current taste, and in developing
countries, where a significant part of today's torture takes
place, they hinder rather than help the discovery of truth,
because of their high rate of failure. There's nothing better
than the old well-proven kicking the shit out of someone,
and all you need for that are a hard fist and a solid iron-
tipped boot . . . as long as it's possible to sew it to measure,
so you don't stub your toe. You kick the shit out of people
and then you rummage around and take what you need.
Simple, right? And yet nothing more accomplished has
been invented so far. People can fly to the moon, and
meanwhile . . .

"London, you say?" said the man with the scarred face.
"An interesting and very significant comparison."

"Unlike me," I said promptly, "who is well known for not
pushing myself forward, and giving preference to—"

EVER GREEN IS . . .

69
▾

"Shut up," responded one of the thugs, and in order to give greater emphasis to his words, he pushed the pole of ice with his fist, to the point that it was swaying dangerously.

gullet Have you ever been on a swing with your hands and feet tied? Not to mention that the insatiable gullet—and that's still too weak a word—of a tub full of sulfuric acid is gaping beneath you? And its toxic fumes, *nota bene,* are importunately attacking your delicate mucous membranes? While the sensitive epidermal layers in your erogenous zones are being anesthetized by the cold emanating from the pole of ice? That, my dear friend, is what they call a happening! That kind of situation cannot be arranged by any of today's charlatans; it could only be created by the greatest artist of life itself all time—life itself. We can only admire it sincerely and with deep respect. For me, at least, tied up and hanging on the pole of ice, nothing else was left. My enthusiasm for the inexhaustible richness of life, for its unrepeatability (sliding off the slippery, icy surface, I realized that perhaps I would never repeat this situation ever again in my life), grew within me at every moment and ultimately it could not be suppressed.

Thanks "Thanks!" I called out in a powerful voice, turning to my benefactors. "Thanks, friends!" And simply with those words, I raised up my hands to heaven . . . well, not all the way there, but I can say without exaggeration that I touched the vaulted ceiling of the royal dungeon with the tips of my fingernails. It's lucky that it wasn't wooden, or I would have gotten a splinter, and that really stings under your fingernails.

Dear friend, on this earth a person is either a hammer or an anvil. In the given situation, I was closer to an anvil, but at the moment when my entire body—except my appendix, which had been removed when I was a child—was straining upward in order to feed on the pastures of the universe, so to speak, the rope with which my legs were tied broke, the inertia of the swinging pole of ice ejected me,

and then, as if by the wave of a magic wand, I was trans-
formed into a hammer.

8

This life, dear friend, set many tasks before me, required
me to adopt the most various forms and disguises; but I
say this without a shade of bitterness, as you are certainly
noticing, because if today I look back on my long period of
active duty, I repeat along with the poet Neruda: Every job
I happened to do, I enjoyed.

It wasn't always very easy, believe me: for example, when
I was a snake-catcher in Styria. The countryside didn't exactly
abound in snakes. Or when I ran a house of ill repute in
Beirut. Have you ever been to Beirut? Don't bother, or you
may find yourself unwittingly running my former business:
"X. and Sons, Finest Selection and Quality." Gentlemen
prefer blondes. All that talk about the export of girls on a
grand scale is overstated, but in the brothels of Tangiers
there was also a great demand for boys. When I had to be
an undercover agent in Beirut and had to choose a cover for
myself, it seemed to be that the occupation of a pimp sell-
ing young boys would be most useful. Every tenth inhabitant of Lebanon is a millionaire, and I myself wasn't among
the first nine either.

Those glittering Lebanese summers! Not a drop falls
from May to September. The everlasting snow on the
mountains above Beirut is blindingly sparkling. You can't
take a step without sunglasses. If you have a bit of sense,
not even with sunglasses, because the taxi drivers ask only
for 2 piasters per kilometer. In view of the fact that Lebanon
measures only 4,300 square miles, you can cross the whole
country for peanuts. I spent my time, however, in simpler
pleasures. Mornings on a sun-parched beach under the
Boulevard Jenah, then a rich lunch in the hotel . . . I especially liked tabbouleh. . . . Have you ever tried it? You take

300 grams of bulgur wheat, crush it in a mortar, then add 150 grams of fresh onion, the same amount of green onion, blend it all. . . . I know, you prefer Wiener schnitzel anytime, don't you? And afternoons at the ideal ski slopes in Bhandoum, 24 kilometers from Beirut, 1,300 meters above sea level. And as it turned out, unfortunately, only 200 meters from Israel's greatest spy, Jerzy Stummdorfer-Wisniewsky, real name Yehiel Blum. He worked in a summer resort—or rather, should I say, winter resort?—as a ski instructor. Do you indulge in dance and sport? I did. With a childhood spent in the dismal conditions of the collapsing Austro-Hungarian Empire, and as a youth fully occupied with active service to my country, my ski skills were far from perfect, and I had decided to improve them without delay. My instructor was none other than Yehiel Blum, a renowned expert. But he saw right through me—a few of his professional tricks were enough, and they were carrying me in a little crate with the inscription SAUERKRAUT across the border. As I said, I enjoyed every job I happened to do, as long as I wasn't sauerkraut. Do you know how they make sauerkraut? With their feet, and in Israel, not even their bare feet. Those were difficult moments. The worst of the whole thing was that they were all Jews there. Theoretically, one can reconcile oneself with that, of course, but when you see it with your own eyes. . . .

I was also a housekeeper for the Archbishop Makarios III of Cyprus. A holy man! He didn't have the slightest idea about sex, and when he sneaked into my little room, nothing could stop him. We had a great time together; to this day I still dream about him sometimes. The only thing that oppressed me in that particular situation was my corset. But one should just take life as it is, corsets and all. I remember even worse moments. Whenever I was coming up with some plan, I suffered just like a woman in childbirth. I'm not the only one to say this; it was first said by Napoleon, who certainly knew about his own parturitions.

I met with one of the most psychologically and physically demanding tasks in a certain backwater of the world. Have you ever heard of Slovakia? It doesn't surprise me. I would say that it's a godforsaken country, but first I'd have to be sure that God had ever known about it in the first place. Right next to the heart of Europe, in the subendo- cardial region, so to speak. So it's no surprise that, for me, Slovakia became a matter of the heart. A diamond doesn't rot in the ground. Naturally the same can't be said of you. Imagine the Transylvanian Alps, only curving the other direction, and you have a clear picture of Slovakia. The whole land area of Slovakia belongs to the West Carpathi- ans, which we can—but we don't need to, I should add, just to calm you down—divide into two basic parts: an older one, the inner Carpathians, and a newer one, the outer Carpathians. The inner Carpathians arose in the Jurassic era during the main mountain-forming Alpine phase, which forcefully shaped their outer form.

What I'm speaking about took place in Upper Hungary, as they refer to the already-mentioned region in official publications. Slovaks themselves, a primitive and scientifi- cally underdeveloped nation, use the local term Slovakia; only certain university-educated individuals proudly declare themselves Upper Hungarians. Austria-Hungary—because that's the country we're talking about—thanks to its well- thought-out national politics, was called the prison of nations. My homeland is all humankind, a world of ideas and historical movements . . . but I have, I don't hide it, my own favorite places. Slovakia is relatively not so far from the sea, since its most eastern point, Královský Chlmec, lies only 680 kilometers from the Baltic, Adriatic, and Black Seas, not to mention the Mediterranean, or the Atlantic and Pacific Oceans. Thanks to this location, jet streams flowing from the sea can easily influence the weather and climate. Due to its elevation, dense forestation, and great distance from the scorching lowlands, Orava remains the coldest region of Slovakia even in the summer—16.1 degrees Celsius in July. It rains heavily in spring and fall, but climatic conditions are not particularly difficult at all. The best time for any warring endeavor: May to October.

Pressburg, which for lack of a better name is sometimes also referred to as Bratislava, is the city that Napoleon's excel-General lent officer General Dessaix called one of the most beauti-Dessaix ful in the Austrian empire. The average July temperature, measured at the airport, is 22 degrees Celsius.

Slovakia is well known for its meteorological stations. One very successful station in the last century (starting in 1872) was the station in Nedanovce, which the nobleman G. Friesenhof rebuilt as an agro-meteorological one, the first one of its kind in Hungary. He published his own agro-1882 meteorological monthly (beginning in 1882) with a fourteen-day forecast. Another instrument of the nobility, serving to brainwash the working masses. Health conditions are more or less favorable; only in the German regions of the mountains in central Slovakia were people undersized and ailing, since from their arrival in that land they had lived on mining, and whole generations were more often under the earth than above. In mountainous regions, as in Slovakia, and also in Subcarpathian Ruthenia, people devoted themselves to alcohol. Even after the fall of the empire, they drank methyl alcohol and became cretins—although they paid the Jewish shopkeepers everything they had for this poison. The fever which originates in the swamps around the flooding Tisa and Hornad Rivers is endemic. Epidemics are only isolated, however. There isn't a complete lack of drinking water, although it often doesn't rain for several weeks; the dwarfed grain shows signs of this. In the lowlands, the drinking water is no good; it causes diarrhea.

I'll mention, only for clarification, that our synopticians differentiate twenty-five types of weather, out of which ten are anticyclonal and fifteen cyclonal, according to the locations of the high- and low-pressure fronts, respectively. I think that's enough to give you a basic picture of Slovakia. The integrated barnyard of an integrated Europe. At the time of the sugar-beet campaign, 30 percent of the length of Slovak rivers, i.e., around 1,432 kilometers, are harmfully polluted, a decent European average, which not even an industrially more advanced country should be ashamed of. 1,432 km

The same thing can be said, with a certain exaggeration, of the Slovaks as a nation. Slovaks, if I may characterize them in the words of one of their own, are like women, eager for praise and pleasure; they all want to live peacefully and comfortably. But it doesn't quite work out for all of them—and this is also thanks to my modest endeavor.

Now let's go beneath the surface. The study of spiritual cultures cannot be done without a deep psychological knowledge of Christian doctrine and its influence on people. Moreover, Slovakia lies on the European intersection of cultures, which due to their own ideologies had a political effect as well. For example, in Germany they systematically study phenomena of a religious character among primitive nations for practical colonial needs. Extensive German colonies are the living proof of the need of such studies. intersection of cultures

The Germans gave the world Goethe and Karl May, the Slovaks Murgaš and Karol Kolman. Murgaš gave the world the radio, Karol Kolman the anthem of abstinence. It was in April of 1923, when the majestic and clear tones of the anthem rang out for the first time: "Brothers, raise the flag of abstinence!" Have you heard it? anthem of abstinence

"Brothers, raise the flag of abstinence! No assault can overcome us, when the Lord is with us." Incidentally, here you have the first written proof that God is—or at least in April 1923 he was—an abstainer. On the other hand, a certain ambiguity of the formulation and rules of dialectics inspires the assumption that in other circumstances God was or could have been a drunkard. After all, God is all-powerful, not to mention the fact that he doesn't exist. Do you believe in God? Well, there you have it. April 1923

EVER GREEN IS . . .

"No matter that we are but a few, forward and onward let us go! When the fight for truth arose, who resisted it?" This part is marked with abstinent mysticism—it can't be understood on the first listening; thus it's repeated four more times. As is the custom in modern works, it raises questions rather than offering answers.

"Holy purity and morality shall be our shield! Despite the world's laughter and scorn, we want to live morally but a few and ethically. No matter that we are but a few. . . ." Objectively speaking, we should admit that their numbers did not grow after 1923; on the contrary, they thinned out— even Karol Kolman passed away. The fact that Kolman died in oblivion speaks volumes for the Slovak character. Slovaks know how to forget even the greatest wrongs. In the shell of every anger, a kernel of forgiveness is sleeping. Nowhere, I guess, was there such a deeply rooted hatred of Jews as there was right among the Slovak people, who used the pejorative term "Yid" for them. Really, you didn't know that? You're just getting to know Slovaks and I can see that you're already taking a liking to them. And nevertheless, when a Jew became worse off than the Slovaks were used to, they'd take pity on him and say that "he's been a bad man, but still, we're not going to kill him." This peculiarity in the Slovak character is referred to profession-vaiató ally as vacillation, from the Latin vaiató, vaiatáre." The so-called dovishness in the Slovak character is very question-able, and the opinion that it is even an innate quality is completely untrue by today's understanding.

"Though the whole world may wallow in drunkenness, we shall direct our flight to heaven's heights." I'm not talk-ing about us, don't look at me so uncomprehendingly, but Kolman's abstainers. And since you're already standing, pour me some more; you've heard that they don't have anything against that—for them "the whole world may wallow in drunkenness," no matter what. And to continue: "Black malignancy must perish, the truth will rise again: time will reveal the abstainers' respect and glorious brightness." We, glorious brightness it seems . . . yes, so hand me that glass . . . we will be delivered from that. All this thunder, all these fireworks will be only for the abstainers and the others will just get shit.

Let's drink to the health of the Slovaks. The problems that the Slovak people had to solve in their Central European homeland for one and a half millennia, with all the resources at their disposal, were not inconsiderable. For example, during weddings in Nedec, the mother of the Nedec bridegroom ran to meet the bride's party with a kolach, or hard pastry, with which she hit the bride in the head; she had to break it apart into four pieces and throw those pieces among the gathering, and they fought over every piece. Thus weddings would last for a week or even longer, so the kolach would be hard enough. The fights between the bearers of the national fortune also took their time. Later the mother-in-law ran into the bedroom; the bride ran after her and tried to overtake the mother-in-law running around the table. It's hardly surprising that in Slovakia there seem to be far fewer mothers-in-law per one thousand 1,000 inhabitants inhabitants than in other European countries; for example, in that notorious, above-mentioned Germany. The past must step aside for the future. A bastard of reality. A posthumous child of lust.

We dance on the bones of our ancestors. That isn't necessarily a reproach, but on the other hand, why not say it: it commits us to a certain gracefulness. Slovak women fulfill their obligations on this point with more than good measure. I don't want to cause you eventual disappointment, but the most beautiful Hungarian women are actually Slovaks. Such cases aren't as rare as you may think. The best Bratislava rolls, or *pajgle,* are produced in Vienna, the best frankfurters in Prague. In Latin, that's called a *genius loci.* Yes, and *génius loci* if I may return to my theme, you'll find the greatest number of those *genia loci,* or local geniuses, in Slovakia. In fact, you wouldn't find any other kinds of geniuses there.

I was compelled by circumstances to be engaged for a long time as a *genius loci* and I could speak about that for hours on end. Of course, that's only one of the aspects of my genius. The living proof of my activities at the time is some legends preserved in the oral tradition to this day, and a lady professor in the department of history in Bratislava, which in Hungarian is actually called Pozsony. Do you speak Hungarian? You are as many people as the languages you speak. This common saying has a single regrettable exception: You can speak Hungarian twenty times over, and yet you still won't stop being Hungarian.

Pozsony

Don't think that I'm prejudiced. Nationalism interests me only as a donkey that helps to turn the wheel of history. "*Jeszcze Polska nie zginela,*" sing the patriotic Poles, "Poland has not yet perished," and they think the only reason it hasn't perished was to make them happy. The Romanian king Carol II, and I say this on the basis of a personal interview, supposed that the historical mission of the Romanian nation, the meaning, so to speak, of its existence, was the preservation and expansion of Romance culture in the inhospitable regions of the Balkans, and so far the only lasting thing that has remained from the Romanians is *bryndza* cheese—especially the May variety, which lasts the longest—and the ruins of Povazsky Castle in Slovakia. The Germans are always all that *Sturm und Drang, Drang nach Osten, Drang nach Westen, Dichtung und Wahrheit,* and in all that tussling and scuffling, they aren't able to realize that their mission is to serve as an exclamation mark of history, as a warning example of what extremes are best avoided. The Austrians bet everything on a single horse, and it turned out to be an ox. Before they recovered, the glory and greatness of Austria were gone. Today the Austrian nation is only an optical illusion, a rainbow of sweet colors, which in a little summer shower can be glimpsed across the Danube from the top of Kobyla Hill in Moravia. An eloquent witness to the fall of Austria is the fact that the

Carol II

Sturm und Drang

Kobyla

best school in Vienna is Spanish, and it is attended by horses. The only thing uniting the Swiss is the Central European time zone and the common desire to pass a thousand years of history without any accidents. Just think, a nation that reckons the quality of a cheese according to the number of empty holes in it! That kind of refinement was what doomed Ancient Rome.

The Swiss are no dummies; they will not pull the mill-stone, they'd rather hang on there and ride on it; they don't have any idea that they are only a sack of sand, which history will throw out of the gondola without regret at the first big decrease. And the French! If de Gaulle hadn't had such a big nose, the French and their culture would have been forgotten a long time ago. You'll see that in a few years the only thing left of them will be the proper name "French," which will be used purely to refer to a certain type of condoms and colognes for advertising purposes. And so on. All nations want to plow a deep furrow in the history of humanity, they want to surpass themselves, but so far, they haven't been able to reach knee-high; only Slovaks, the children of God, see the meaning and fulfillment of their existence in the simple fact that they exist. Who else knows how to have such childlike pleasure: "Two hundred years have gone by already, and we're still here! There must be something behind it! We're still here, and that can't just be an accident!" And then, full of enthusiasm, they determine a clear goal: "Let's keep right on existing!"

I can't help it, I like them. Slovak women! Blood and milk! Well, as for the blood, we're not cannibals, but that milk! There's so much of it, and what quality! From this point of view, Slovakia could be called the udder of Europe. The milk of German or English mothers, and I won't even mention Americans, is just a series of factory goods in comparison with the Slovak variety. Concretely, my lady profes-sor—but when we first met, she was a simple herdess of cows . . . the word "simple" may have a pejorative tinge in

de Gaulle

Let's keep right on existing!

series of goods

your eyes, but it pales in comparison with actuality. If I were to call her an imbecile, I couldn't help feeling that I was unjustifiably flattering her. I'll grant you this—for a shepherdess, or rather cowherdess, she was quite brave.

The fate of poor Slovak girls—*nota bene,* idiots—was rather gloomy in the time of developing capitalism. Their long days were spent in the magnificent solitude of the mountains—only the cows paid attention, so that she wouldn't wander off somewhere. You have to add the droit du seigneur on the first night—and of course the right to a second or third night, and so on, because during the historical process, this feudal privilege was democratically divided among all citizens. Just to make the situation even more poignant, what the poor shepherdess was lacking in common sense was more than made up for in beauty. It must be said that the generous hand of nature placed a bonus on the most-exposed places. Suffice it to say that in the times when the exploitation of one man by another still flourished in Slovakia—incidentally, it was the most widely practiced form of enterprise—the dear fellow citizens made a list (similar to those we see today in apartment houses with a common laundry room) which included everyone from the mayor to a common beggar, not to mention the village stud-bull.

A sad story. In the period of which we're speaking, the fate of the simple cowherdess was already decided. Deep shocks of a primarily—but not exclusively—mental nature caused a malfunction, which is referred to in the textbooks of sexology with the term "vaginismus." In a word, she didn't like copulation at all. If I may express my opinion—and you certainly won't prevent me—I wasn't even surprised. The principle of free choice was grossly violated, and the pleasures that were to compensate for this were of dubious quality. The missionary position, practiced in a monotonous and unimaginative manner, which arrived in this country with Saints Cyril and Methodius a millennium ago. . . .

Marginal notes: droit du seigneur / village stud-bull / Cyril and Methodius

You shouldn't think that I'm overstating this in the least; I'm speaking on the basis of my own experience. Umm . . . you know what I mean.

Do you play chess? That's sensible; at least you don't reinforce your inferiority complex at every step. But I suppose you know what a pawn is, at least. I don't mean the ones who actually labor, but the kind that are manipulated. A pawn who moves from E2 to E4 doesn't need to know that this is a Spanish opening. . . . I'm sure you don't know this yourself; in this direction I'm not overestimating you in the least. . . . In a certain sense it is actually desirable that the pawn shouldn't know that he would be sacrificed in another move. Well, this "pawn doctrine" ruled in the [doctrine] counterespionage of the young Czechoslovak state, whether from necessity or from conviction. After all, we are all pawns in the hands of God. I say this only as proof that the above-mentioned words weren't meant as a criticism.

To make a long story short, this crippled cowherdess, who gazed listlessly at the swarms of flies on the cow's tail, figured on the payroll of the Ministry of National Defense [MND] under the code name Stella II. Being oneself is sometimes difficult, even impossible; in her case, however, there was nothing easier, because just for technical reasons she couldn't be anything else, and in addition, to make her happiness complete, they even paid her for it. Even the cows, which surrounded her like picturesque stage props, were on the ministry's supply payroll, and when one of them, out of sheer boredom or desperation, separated from the herd and decided to begin an independent life, they simply entered it under the column of war losses and left it to its fate.

I see it in your face, that you would have liked that kind of job . . . that you would have fully developed your natural talents, you, the Napoleon of the forest hideaways. These days it is done differently—without passing a basic [technical] technical exam, you wouldn't be allowed to tend the cows. [exam]

Even this path to a career has been closed off to you. As for Stella II, the simple Slovak professor . . . the majority of Slovak women professors are simple; it's really one of the nice things about them. If you want a governess, pick an English one, if a philosopher, a German one, if a cognac, a French one, and a woman professor, a Slovak one.

I don't recall at the moment what it was all about; I guess it was just the removal of a certain general named Pištikam or Štefanko or something like that. I even remember that they paid me for it in marks. Slovakia had become a point of intersection for European interests, and when the European interests intersected, of course I couldn't be absent. I was then in the bloom of youth. . . . I guess you're thinking that the bloom of my youth has already taken up a long stretch of time, but I must warn you that if I were to com-

perennial pare myself to a blossom, I was a perennial blossom—in contrast to that General Štefánik (why, I've just remembered it) who faded very quickly, because, if I were to state it more clearly, he was plucked out by the hand of the Holy Gardener. Do you believe in God? Neither do I, but General Štefánik believed, and that kind of poetic metaphor certainly could have helped him to reconcile himself to inexorable reality.

By the way, he was the first Slovak French general, and the last one to this day—at the time, the Slovak army did not yet exist, and so he had to be named a general by the French, who in this way cleverly masked the espionage character of his mission. How the Slovaks just loved him! I mean after his death; while he was alive, he was mostly loved by Italian women. . . . Yes, he became their favorite plaything, and so it is to this day: if the Slovaks behave, then give them Štefánik, let them play, and if they misbehave, then take him away from them.

How much that general without an army longed to make history—and all in vain!—while the simple Slovak woman Stella II—it is, incidentally, a very widely used name in Slovakia—was, so to speak, pushed into it against her will.

she had gone through the school of hard knocks—it was, incidentally, the only school she had gone through, other than the first grade of a Hungarian elementary school—and she had learned not to take the Ten Commandments very seriously. Yes, when I consider it, I don't think she even knew all of them. One thing is certain: It cannot be said that the seven deadly sins would have been disgusting to her. 10 Commandments 7 deadly sins

Do you know the seven deadly sins? I thought so immediately. Perhaps from your everyday experience. I don't know whether education that consists of only lacunae can still be called an education.

It's enough to say that hearing my exclamation "Yodelay-ee-ho," the cowherdess pulled up her skirt without a word or a single look around. From her behavior, I concluded that Czech tourists were not completely unknown in this region. Oh yes, the Slovaks, an unlucky nation, for a millennium they bemoaned their bondage. . . . Do you know how to bemoan? So bemoan for me! What? Man, that sounds like a marmot's mating call. It's clear that you have never bemoaned, I mean truly, from the heart: Oooooooohhhh. . . . Even I have already gotten a little out of practice, unlike the Slovaks; they never had the opportunity to get out of practice, because they bemoaned constantly for a thousand years. While Foolish Johnny was fighting a nine-headed dragon, Slovakia, a circumspect maiden, had already unbuttoned her gown. She sang and made daisy chains, waiting without greater interest for the battle to end. She knew beforehand that regardless of the battle's outcome, her rape would inevitably follow. ooooooohhhh

And so it was, as I say, for a thousand years. Of course they did not do it for free. You would not, as I know you, have bemoaned even an hour for free, although, frankly speaking, I don't know what sort of dunce would give you even a nickel for your bemoaning. 1,000 years

In a word, so I don't digress, the dear cowherdess was proof that a millennium of raping had left its traces, that it blended with Slovak blood. There are, *entre nous,* more difficult jobs and less rewarding ones. I think that a Slovak must like being raped, because during it, you lie on your back and, if you like, maybe even with your hands above your head. It was really the Slovaks, of all the European

Confucius nations, who were the first to transform the old Confucian wisdom: If you can't fight off a rape, lie back and enjoy it and try to make the most of it, to transform it into (not into a cliché; don't confuse me, you idiot), to transform it into—you see, now this word has slipped my mind. Well, it doesn't matter.

Have you ever been raped by anyone? So that's just waiting for you; it's good when a person still has something to look forward to. Today's youth lives too fast, in my opinion. I don't mean race cars; it doesn't even bother me that they drive buses to school; it might be faster if they

scooter went by scooter. Now, where were we? Oh, in the fragrant, sunny, lost meadow under the Blatnica castle, in the lap of . . . I know, I promised you I would stop bringing up nature. And yet I must say something pretty, jingling, gleaming with ornamentation, like a careful mother who shows her little boy the stars, so he doesn't notice that some drunkard is urinating on the sidewalk.

Dreadful is the loneliness of a man commissioned for secret tasks in the world of simple everyday things, among people who drink warm foamy milk from a mug and wipe their grubby hands on their trouser legs. Still more dreadful is the loneliness of a Czech tourist with a backpack and

thick thick kneesocks in a world of shot glasses and thick wads
kneesocks of spit soaked with tobacco. And I, as if that first loneliness were not enough for me, on the advice of my employers I took it upon my shoulders—they were powerful, and even now . . . don't you want to touch them?—and took over that second, harder one.

Were it not for that loneliness, which distorts one's viewpoint so you see even those closest to you as if through the reverse side of a pair of binoculars, that loneliness which brands you in your own eyes with the mark of Cain . . . good, isn't it? The artist in me, yes indeed; don't look at me like that, an artist is hidden here within my breast—don't you believe me? Two more could easily fit in such a breast—the artist in me is like Božena Nemcová's grand- B.N. mother, always prepared to jump over a fence for a colorful feather . . . especially someone else's fence. Have you heard of Božena Nemcová's grandmother? No, you're too young for that, but at least Božena Nemcová herself. . . . Too young for that too? Božena Nemcová was the Czech Mata Hari, in the days when the Dutch had not yet even dreamed of Mata Hari. It would be more correct to say that Mata Hari was the Dutch Božena Nemcová, but who nowadays, may I ask you, pays attention to correct speech? Maybe some linguist driven to write a language column.

To make a long story short, in the middle of that meadow, so green and lush (unlike myself—I'm almost never drunk), among those sweet bubbling brooks and the quiet lowing of cows, I glimpsed a provocatively glittering well-built pair of legs. They looked white at a distance (especially when, as I've already mentioned, I was looking around with the wrong end of the binoculars, which was the usual custom among Czech tourists at the time) . . . temptingly white and innocent. Everyone carries his own cross, and if the simple Slovak cowherdess Stella II, in the dismal conditions of developing—by the way, very slowly developing—capitalism, suffered from vaginismus, she still could have congratulated herself that she hadn't fared worse, when we take into account the number of her copulations. . . . In a randomly selected location of central Java, they examined 6,000 people, and out of these, 3,229, that is, 54 percent, had one or more venereal diseases, and out of 54% that number, 2,990 had one, 227 had two, and 12 individuals had three venereal diseases at the same time . . . so if the simple cowherdess Stella II was stricken with vaginismus,

I myself was suffering at that time from the disease known
—though perhaps not to you—by the name of priapism,
and the long fast didn't help my condition any.

It was almost becoming a Greek tragedy. We have each
carried our own cross, and done it so carelessly that we've
been hit over the head by it. But this is not an easy game
at all. Religion is, naturally, the opium of the masses, but I
have to acknowledge: Lugging a cross, as Christ did, and
up a hill at that, is a job for a longshoreman. Have you ever
been a longshoreman? I tell you, I've always been and still
am happy that I was never a longshoreman. Anyway, there's
always some kind of odd job for the likes of us. For example,
dynalkol   that affair with the *dynalkol* . . . do you think I would have
undertaken such a task if there hadn't been the prevailing
conviction, in the postwar depression of the time, that there
would never be another world war?

So I underestimated the danger when, in a rather carefree manner—only bothered by my trousers, which I had,
from that very impatience, unbuttoned a little too early—
I started running across through the meadow. I said across,
not with a cross; the cross, which I mentioned earlier, was
only a metaphor. Before you could count to three—no, I'll
lower it for you, so you don't have the impression that I was
1, 2, 3!   a cripple: Before you could count to two. . . . Do you
know how to count to two? Do you swear on the lives of
your parents that you do? I immediately thought that you
were an orphan. Well, well, I believe you.

In short, in a moment I ran two hundred meters—in
view of the numerous cow droppings, there were more or
200 m   less two hundred meters of hurdles that separated me, as
of hurdles   (blinded by passion) I mistakenly supposed, from the eager
cowherdess. I had omitted a romantic prelude under the
pressure—if I no longer want to speak of other, more concrete pressures—of the circumstances. In that country, they
are not so particular about such things, and I think I probably would have confused my dear cowherdess by my refined

art, rather than transporting her into a romantic ecstasy. I wasn't even slowed down when the laces of my hiking boots came untied—when I hurry, you know, they always get in knots—I bent down over the maiden, who blinked her eyes and sweetly whispered with her sensual red lips. . . . Later I learned that in similar situations she always counted to one from 1 to 100 hundred in her mind, in order not to start an ill-considered show of resistance, which doesn't bring any results, apart from certain bruises.

Si non è vero, è bene trovato, as the ancient Romans used to say. The little cowherdess had difficulties counting to ten, and speaking of the mind in connection with her is the same as mentioning a smokestack in a conversation about a sailboat. Yet the fact remains that her sensually shaped lips moved silently but attractively, and if you had a little imagination—in your case, that doesn't come into consideration—you could imagine they were calling your name. As for me, in contrast to God, it was certainly not in vain, because immediately thereafter I tried to penetrate the temple of delight, whose gates, as I supposed, were wide open.

But how great was my surprise when the envoy of my envoy desire—good, isn't it? I came up with it myself—met with of desire an unexpected difficulty! Well, how great do you think it was? Do you give up? Coward. Enormous, of course, and unpleasant, but in that moment not even the greatest surprise in the world could have stopped me. I accepted the explanation which first offered itself, and I spat this word in her face like a curse: "Virgin!" Virgin!

Fortunately, she didn't understand me, because otherwise she would have been seized with an irresistible attack of laughter, and if it had seized her, I wouldn't have been able to seize her myself. Because of this, however, my spirits did not sag, and what is more important, neither did anything else—I plunged with new élan to the attack.

Perhaps I don't need to say that when I plunge into an attack with élan (whether new or not), hardly anything

resists me. She didn't resist me either. I felt that the gates
of the temple were allowing me in—a glorious moment, the
moment of triumph! Flooded with the feeling of victory—it
had to do, as you see, with the relatively rare case of liquid
feeling—I did not even realize right away that the gates had
only opened briefly and soon, when I had penetrated inside,
closed again.

What I had not realized right away, I realized after a
moment, and more intensely. Have you ever slammed your
finger in a door? You have? Often? So you see what I mean,
and now we have to take into consideration the well-known
fact that a finger is not the most sensitive part of the human
body. You think it's the sole of the foot, you say? You probably have that from those stories about the Wild West and
the Near East by Karl May, and from the worst of them.
I'm sure you remember the adventures of Hadzi Halef
Omar, or Kara Ben Nemsi . . . it doesn't surprise me that
you were hooked on his books. It's bad enough that he was
a German and a thief, but for pity's sake, such an inept
one, who gave his students some busywork to distract them
and then crept out into the corridor to look through their
coat pockets, and even let himself be caught! Someone like
that inevitably abuses literature in order to treat his own
complexes. Did you notice how well his characters, like Old
Shatterhand the paleface, not to mention Winnetou the
Indian and the grizzly bear, knew how to sneak?

Karl May took the old superstition of the sole of the
foot as the most sensitive spot on the human body from
third-rate novels about the Turkish invasion of Hungary.
But I, when declaring something, do not rely on literature,
but use my own experience. Having your fingernails pulled
out with red-hot pliers—if I may only mention the first
thing that sprang to mind—having your fingernails pulled
out is a relatively unpleasant affair, but if they also took
red-hot pliers and pulled out your teeth, which are surely
predestined by nature to be pulled out, it wouldn't be

delightful either. In that direction, I am a defender of the simple quantitative theory, and I believe that if they pulled out your fingers with red-hot pliers, it would be even more painful . . . not to mention the pain you would feel if they took red-hot pliers and pulled off your whole hand.

But the goal of torture, naturally, is not to cause pain for its own sake; pain must not be wasted, and it is well known—at least well enough to me—that within a certain unit of time, a person is able to consume and/or process only a certain quantum of pain: the rest escapes, so to speak, into the ether. Those are these useless faintings during interrogation. Something like that cannot happen to an experienced chief torturer. An experienced chief torturer does not chief torturer go full force right away, so therefore he starts with the nails, in order to leave a certain reserve, and only an extraordinarily naive person, if I don't want to say feeble headed—frankly speaking, not that I do not want; quite the contrary, I'm greatly tempted to—only such a person can draw the conclusion that nails are the most sensitive part of the human body. Believe me, that's a dead end, the path of least resis- dead end tance—to suppose that the part of the body that hurts me just now is the most sensitive! Finally, if by chance a flowerpot falls on your head, you will be ready to swear that the head is the most sensitive part of the body, although— at least in your case—you couldn't be further from the truth!

And I won't even mention certain utilitarian aspects, that is, the question of the further use of the interrogated man, which should also be taken into consideration. Thus the Turks, who traveled on horses, punished their soldiers by Turks beating them on the soles of their feet . . . because if they had beaten them on the backside, the next day they would not have been able to continue the journey, and that would actually have lowered their fighting ability. Yes, and perhaps while you had, as I judge from the saliva that is running down your chin—dry yourself off; it's not very appetizing—while you had in mind that traditional image of the

voluptuously lounging Turkish bey whose underage servants
scratch his heels, I must tell you again, for the umpteenth
time—solving logical problems has always suited my rich
fantasies more than mechanical calculations—to say that
sensual smile you once again have not understood anything: the sensual
smile on the bey's face is not an expression of momentarily experienced, current pleasure, but the anticipated pleasure, that is to say, the advance bliss. But it's difficult to
speak with the blind about colors and with you about
pleasure . . . no, don't confuse it with that pleasant feeling
you experience when you pick some dried snot out of
your nose with your finger.

Well, let it be. Underage servants . . . curly cherubic
heads . . . in that direction we still have something to learn
from the Turks: hundreds of years of a sharpened aesthetic
sense. . . . Scratching the heels makes the blood flow to
the sole of the foot, and when it comes to the actual act of
pleasure, it is more blissful and lasts longer, since the
blood has to move to the proper place. Up to now it is
simply a technical thought, a practical application of the
American laws of physiology, the American approach, so to speak; but
approach only a nation with such a long cultural tradition as the Turks
could have come up with the idea that the heels should be
scratched by rosy-cheeked boys with smooth milky skin.
But not even a Turk, I'm sure of it, would have come up
with a way to free himself from the merciless embrace I
unexpectedly found myself in without damaging at the same
time one of the most precious organs—but why hesitate,
let's say it openly—that is, the most precious organ, with
which nature has endowed man. I soon understood—my
quick wits were already proverbial back in my school days—
that the solution to this problem required more time, and
I decided—I don't like to do more than one thing at the
same time; it distracts one's attention needlessly—to finish the thing that had brought me to the cowherdess in
the first place.

Nowadays any small-town movie-theater projectionist could give lectures on interpersonal communication, but in my youth, this theoretical field was still lying fallow. It wouldn't have even occurred to anyone to search for other, hidden meanings of words; it was more profitable to search for cranberries or blueberries. Today it's just the opposite. It's true that in those days there were also more of those cranberries and blueberries, and more people believed in God, or nature, if you like: if the meanings are hidden, they thought, maybe that's how it should be; maybe it's better that way. And believe me, it was. Do you believe me? That's a mistake; our kind of people must not believe anyone. In fact, even I wasn't always able to avoid this mistake. For example, during the minor but important part I played in ruining the experiments with *dynalkol,* the advisers of the Vacuum Oil Co. had given me the disguise of a Czech tourist, including a Czech-to-Slovak dictionary; I believed they had chosen this option in their own best interest. As it turned out, the very opposite was true.

Czech-to-Slovak dictionary

I don't want to bore you with a prolonged sociological-historical analysis of the situation in the region of the former Upper Hungary right after the end of the First World War. The new Czechoslovak state was still a newborn baby then, so to speak, and there were enough guardians around who were willing not only to change its diapers but also to fill its bottle—what they would fill it with, of course, was open to speculation. Who knows why everyone thought that the simple Slovak folk were the most suitable ones to make drunk. It's true that when the Slovaks, after a thousand years of bemoaning, were suddenly required to be jubilant about their freedom, they were slightly upset with this new state of affairs. And therefore, Czech tourists began to swarm to Slovakia, whose purpose was to inconspicuously ensure that this jubilation would be spontaneous and for the right cause.

bottle

Those Slovaks who were "mistaken" about this rightful new state of affairs were to have those ideas knocked out of their heads with a few well-aimed punches.

I should note that in August 1919, the territory of Slovakia, which measured 51,689 square kilometers, was inhabited by 1,940,000 Slovaks, 650,000 Hungarians, 143,000 Ruthenians, and 131,000 Germans. And in addition, according to my modest estimate, about a hundred thousand Czech tourists. I was the hundred thousand and first.

1 million, 940 thousand

The vast majority of these Czech tourists were idealists, convinced that they were going to spread culture and enlightenment among the backward Slovak folk. What kind of culture and enlightenment they had in mind is best explained in the writing of a certain Holeček, also a Czech, which was published in the magazine *Bell*. I consider it a unique document in all of human history, which includes a direct insult of God the Father, so I feel that I should cite the text itself:

Holeček

"An ugly episode took place in Slany. On the evening before the national holiday of Jan Hus, around two hundred people rushed to the square and surrounded the plague column, with its Holy Trinity. Suddenly one of them climbed up the column, boxed God the Father's ears a few times on both sides, then shattered his head with a hammer. The crowd of bourgeoisie witnessed this with indifference. The impulse to such vandalism came from a teacher in the local high school."

And as I know the Czechs, the only reason they didn't tear off the feathers of the Holy Spirit was that it flew away just in time. It is completely clear that such manners didn't appeal to the heart of the God-fearing Slovak folk. In the bastion of the Slovak national movement, in Turiec county, the resistance to the sudden rise of Czech tourism gained concrete forms. After all, the Slovaks had had centuries-long experience with foreign tourists, with the Avars, familiarly called Huns, the Tatars, or the Turks. Of course I, the

bastion of the movement

hundred-thousand-and-first Czech tourist, didn't have the slightest inkling of this.

When a stranger comes to Turiec, it is worthwhile for him to look around. I know that now, but I didn't know it then. The whole region was somehow surrounded by high mountains. Strategically, Turiec certainly would have been important, and it was hardly a coincidence that King Béla IV Béla IV found refuge in Turiec when fleeing the Tatars in 1241. And it was hardly a coincidence that I, a simple Czech tourist in 1919, found no refuge in Turiec at all. Regardless of what role the insignificant Slovak idiot-cowherdess code-named Stella II may have played in the plans of the Ministry of Defense, she played a certainly unambiguous role in the plans of her compatriots. They used her as bait, as flypaper, to which disillusioned idealists, bearing culture and full packs of food, would be stuck. They disappeared without a trace —the packs, the culture, and its bearers too.

The movement of watchfulness and vigilance already had a considerable tradition in Turiec. In 1873, for example, 1873 a volunteer firemen's corps was founded in Martin, on the initiative of Jozef Kohut. It was not only a humanitarian association but also a national one. The beginnings of the corps were difficult, and thus each member of the corps had to offer a material sacrifice. The corps struggled for many years with financial difficulties and the indifference of the Hungarian authorities, but the biggest impediment for the authorities was that the language of command for the corps was Slovak. In 1914, nearly the entire corps was drafted, but other eager participants were found, older gentlemen, so the corps continued to function. From this small seed in Martin sprouted the Regional Firemen's Union No. 1 Regional Firemen's Union and from that the huge and powerful Land Firemen's Union. Thus the work of the fathers was not in vain.

While the fathers were bringing their material sacrifice, the sons were busy taking it away. In Blatnica, they had an easy and dependable system for this. In the evening, a man was chosen according to a list—he always went to the pastures to check who had been caught that day by the simple lovely cowherdess. After dark, he would come back, whistling, to the village, with a pack full of food and a fairly new pair of tourist boots. At the time, as I've already mentioned, I didn't know about this extra means of production, but my position—which was, to be more precise, lying down—evoked certain fears in me. I don't confess it gladly, but in the first moment, I even recalled that adolescent trick with a pin. You know, as they say, if you prick a woman unexpectedly with a pin in such a situation, she reflexively relaxes her muscles. A pin was part of the standard equipment of a Czech tourist in Slovakia; there were no problems with that. I'd actually had two pins sent with me—an ordinary one with a blue head and a special one with a red head, which was covered with the rare poison curare. However, the unexpectedness posed a worse problem. The cowherdess was seemingly familiar with such pins, and as soon as she saw a tiny blue head glistening in my fingers, she awoke from her apathy and hit my hand in such a way that the pin, without any sound whatsoever, was sent flying into the grass. Do you know the saying about a needle in a haystack? Well, looking for a pin in tall grass is even worse, especially because the grass was sharp, particularly where I was lying, and one could easily get cut.

So I lost not only the pin but also the moment of surprise, and when I realized that, I decided on a longer but less well traveled and more difficult way, but (as I naively thought) one that would be guaranteed to lead me to my goal. I decided to start with interpersonal communication. Small talk and light conversation remove needless fears and anxieties in one's partner, and create a friendly atmosphere in which not only the soul but also the body can relax. I was especially concerned with the latter.

That type of conversation requires not only natural talent, of which I never had any lack, but also fluency in the

(margin notes:)
extra means of production

r. pin sent = curare

moment of surprise

relevant language, and here some difficulties emerged. The standard equipment of a Czech tourist includes an ignorance of Slovak—it was exactly that which was, so to speak, his sine qua non. In my case, on top of that, in contrast to other Czech tourists, even Czech was not one of my strong points. However, I knew a couple of curses—which, as I soon found out, were rather archaic ones, like "Dash it all!," "Good heavens!," and even the gentle oath "By Jove!," but that was all I could provide. I could also recite perfectly my favorite Czech tongue twister, "Three hundred and thirty-three silver quails flew over three hundred and thirty-three silver rooftops," although it wasn't very clear to me what it meant. Otherwise I had to rely upon my innate feeling for language and upon my already proverbial intuition. But it wouldn't be me if I hadn't prepared for everything. Meanwhile, I pressed tenderly with my three-day-old stubble on the blushing cheeks, covered with smallpox scars, of the lovely cowherdess, while with my free hand I fumbled in my pack for the Czech-to-Slovak dictionary and inconspicuously laid it on the grass.

After leafing through it briefly—I tried to cover the rustling of the paper with clearly audible sighs—I found out that it was an exceptionally competent work, concise and well arranged. In less than two minutes I had looked from *A,* "advert—ad," "advocate—attorney," "aeroplane—airplane," "angry—mad," "aubergine—eggplant," "autumn—fall," to *Z,* "zed—z," "zip—zipper," "zounds—shucks." You can have a light, inconsequential conversation about anything, but I have to confess that the words I found did not strike me as very inspiring.

"Ads for attorneys make me as mad as an eggplant," I said merrily, but I didn't get any response. Frankly speaking, I felt deep in my heart that it wasn't a sentence to break the ice of distrust. But I didn't give up. Feverishly I turned the page and immediately rejoiced. For the dunces among the Czech tourists, there were basic conversational

sine qua non

advert = ad

the ice of distrust

gambits, which could help them to gain the basic necessities of life and the hearts of the simple Slovak folk. On the basis of my own experience, I must add that to gain either one or the other, even in perfect Slovak, was not an easy task. Of all the world's languages, Slovaks best understood the language of money, and at the sound of banknotes rustling, even their hard hearts clearly melted.

After thinking briefly over the topics available, I chose the theme of "weather," a favorite topic of small talk all over the world.

"It shall rain today, perhaps?" I asked, and, made wise by my past failure, I immediately answered myself: "Perhaps a shower is coming; perhaps a thunderstorm. As long as no hail happens to fall!" Alas, with this the theme of weather ended in my conversational handbook. I felt the cowherdess Stella II moving around in surprise under me, so I concluded (thanks to my sharp intuition) that she wasn't used to such extensive verbal expression. I decided to strike while the iron was hot. The most convenient topic, for its brevity and directness, seemed to be the theme "in a pub."

the bill of fare | "Show me the bill of fare!" I told the cowherdess, who was still looking at me in a flabbergasted manner. Her sincere astonishment upset me for a moment. "*Verstehen Sie? Do you understand?*" I said, raising my voice in a manner not customary during small talk. But I immediately contained myself and continued in a kind, friendly tone, which quite often works absolute miracles in interpersonal communication: "Have you got anything to eat or anything to drink?"

the zero point | Although Slovaks are quite well esteemed among gourmets, I have to say sincerely that at the given moment, I didn't care for any answer—I had reached the zero point of demanding anything at all. I considered any answer better than nothing. When the cowherdess/noncowherdess pressed her warm cheek to mine and whispered into my ear—into this one, the right one, as fresh and healthy as a ripe ear of corn, wouldn't you say? It's lovely to whisper into; the most famous beauties of their time have whispered into it, among them even the Princess Liechtenstein and the salesgirl in the leather department at the Brouk and Babka department store—so when she whispered with her sensuous lips, I couldn't avoid a joyful surprise, and my spirit rejoiced. Does your spirit know how to rejoice? I would have thought as much. A person's spirit can rejoice only if he has a spirit at all. Let's drop it; I'd rather skip the part on rejoicing.

Brouk and Babka

"Gimme the money!" was her sweet whisper, and at the same time, a warm breath blew on me, a breath which was expressive testimony that regular dental visits were only a privilege of the upper classes in the old bourgeois Czechoslovak Republic. "You won't need it anymore!"

At the first moment, I was so joyful that I didn't understand her very well. The precondition of real, unfalsified interpersonal communication is that two people must participate in it actively, and this precondition was fulfilled when this human flypaper spoke. The situation, so common today, when one person says something and the other is napping, is undoubtedly an inferior form of communication. Wake up! You say you don't want me to shake you? You're no Sleeping Beauty—I wouldn't wake you up with a kiss!

Sleeping Beauty

Now where were we? Oh, yes! "Dear Colonel," I said in a voice which quivered with passion that was suppressed with effort, "when you touch me, I have the feeling as if I were awakened from a centuries-long sleep, my hitherto sleeping senses. . . ." Nonsense! You're just distracting me with your lack of attention.

Well, in the first moment I didn't believe my own ears. After all, people aren't supposed to believe anything from anyone. Measure it twice and then believe it, as they say.

"What?" I asked in complete confusion, and immediately I translated it handily into Slovak: "Eh?"

"Money!" That time it seemed to me I could hear a slight but distinct resentment in her whisper. "*Baksheesh!* *Lóve! Pengö! Korunky! Lóve! Das Geld!*"

Although around us it was only beginning to get dark, and dusk was still approaching timidly, something began to dawn on me. That's the fate of brilliant people; they have to outrun their time. "That's how it is!" I told myself. From a lack of time, I simply gave up on another attempt at inter-personal communication and decided to act. I caught the dear cowherdess—flypaper that she was, and from my point of view she wasn't particularly comfortable—and, carrying this burden, I ran the five or six steps that separated us from the nearest cow, and thanks to my strength and dexterity, I climbed with her onto the broad bovine back. The view offered to us by this higher place, the slopes of mountains covered with an evening haze, was worthy of the pen of a poet; but there are moments when feelings, however noble, must step aside. And if they won't step aside on their own, they must be energetically pushed away. I did this without hesitation—I kicked the cow's flanks with the heels of my boots, and we galloped away. It was high time. From the forest path below us, we could already hear the whistle of a tourist tax collector.

I'm not going to give you a detailed description of the nine months that I spent with the simple Slovak cowherdess Stella II and Hildegard the cow in the ruins of the ancient Blatnica castle, even if it would, in my description, make the Thirty Years' War seem like school recess. You could find a number of interesting, if not entirely accurate, details in the noteworthy study by Professor Vosahalik, "The Ada-mite Nudists in Turiec," where he proposed the daring hypothesis that the naked Siamese twins in the pristine Slovak forests are directly descended from the soldiers of Jan Jiskra of Brandys, their cultural heritage of a sort. Even the American *National Geographic* magazine featured us in a special article with full photographic coverage. Against our will—certainly against mine, at least—we became a favorite tourist attraction. The members of the local hunters' union, commissioned with the task of maintaining well-stocked game in the region, built us a trim little feeder for the wintertime.

Life in the country has its pleasures, even though Stella II wasn't the kind of woman that a man would take along with him to a desert island. But I was the first Robinson Crusoe in the forests of Turiec; I had to call her, willy-nilly, my girl Friday. All in all, I wouldn't have minded her so much if she had only been Friday, but since she was also Monday, Tuesday, Wednesday, Thursday, Saturday, and Sunday, it literally drove me to despair. I feverishly attempted the most various methods to end this involuntary symbiosis once and for all; I alternated a rough physical pressure—in this case, it would be better to call it anti-pressure—with persuasion; in deep hopelessness I finally grasped—they don't say it for nothing, that a drowning man would even grasp at straws—at the pseudoscientific theories of the Viennese Jew Freud, at the *sogennante Psychoanalyse,* or "so-called psychoanalysis," as he said himself.

For heaven's sake, this preposterous term—psychoanalysis! How is it possible to analyze something that actually doesn't exist! Soon enough I discovered from first-hand experience—and when I say "hand," I don't mean it as a metaphor—the pernicious effects of that modern charlatan's unsubstantiated theories. I jumped, if I may say it so, from the frying pan not even into the fire, but straight into the inferno. The dear cowherdess, marked with long centuries of social and national oppression, immediately and entirely ungroundedly, but in view of the prevailing tone of our conversations quite understandably, began to think that she had a soul. At that moment I realized the symbiosis with the cowherdess's lovely though not particularly clean body was barely bearable, but it could be borne; a symbiosis with her so-called soul, however. . . . Nothing else was

Robinson Crusoe

charlatan

left for me to do but to pitilessly destroy this pathetic monster and replace it with a psychological prosthesis, which I
myself had to make. And that, as you see, has lasted until

Prof. Stella today—thanks to it, Stella II climbed to the heights of
Slovak professorship.

Nowadays, those times appear rather idyllic in my
memory. Specialists call that the optimism of memory, and
it's the only optimism that people in our line of work can
indulge in without hindrance. At the time, however, if I
should speak entirely openly . . . should I? I see that quick
decisions aren't one of your strong suits . . . if I should
speak entirely openly, I didn't have any grounds for optimism. When I gradually tried all methods without success,
I realized that the last refuge, the last path to freedom left

natural to me was the natural method. Fully aware and conscious
method of the consequences, I decided to become a father, hoping
that when the happy time arrived, my little Lluska (as I
already called Stella) would push out along with her fetus,
willy-nilly, my primary sexual organ as well. These days,
parental training is a basic component of high school cur-
ricula, but in those times, taking this step required a lot
of courage and mental independence. I confess that in
a corner of my mind, I also had the fleeting idea that
the government would not leave my tangible contribution
to the official doctrine of a single Czechoslovak nation,

the first real the first real Czechoslovak, unrewarded. But when, after
Czechoslovak nine months, I looked at it close up, I pushed the idea out
of my head. I made a knot on the umbilical cord of the
former cowherdess—in the meantime, with my help, she
had increased her qualifications—so she wouldn't forget
me, and set off down the steep path through the ancient
trees of the forest—alone again . . . all alone . . . utterly
alone. . . .

Let's drop it. Cheap sentimentality disgusts me. A man
in our line of business must be prepared to give up simple
human happiness—in the worst case, even his own—in

the name of a higher cause. There are not, all in all, so many higher causes, or—as I like to call them—ideas. The one that grew the largest in my own heart was the fight for freedom. Freedom for its own sake, in its pure state, so to speak, actually doesn't exist, but the fight for freedom, purely in the fact that it never ends, how many possibilities it offers! What a great possibility of variations, what variety, what richness, how many opportunities for men in our line of work to excel! Because the Olympic slogan also applies to the fight for freedom: "Not to win, but to participate"; on which side is entirely beside the point. Oh, yes, freedom, that proverbial bird in the bush! As soon as you think you have it in your hand, you realize that it's flown right back into the bush to rejoin its friend. Do you love freedom? I love it tremendously, and I really liked Slovaks because of the fact that they love it too. Really, Slovaks are an astoundingly freedom-loving nation; I became convinced of that right in my first days of living among them. After several vain attempts at catching the lovely cowherdess and me in a bear trap, they just shrugged and quoted the famous verses of Ján Kollár: "Worthy of freedom is only he who values all freedom," and they left us alone. Perhaps a certain role was also played by the knowledge that we were much more useful to the locals as a tourist attraction than as a one-time piece of prey, from which nothing could be taken but its bare—and I mean literally bare—life.

Yes, such are the Slovaks. Just so you don't think this is an accidental, subjective impression, I'll introduce the testimony of a Czech officer, who cannot be suspected of blind favor toward Slovaks. As you certainly know, blind favor occurs relatively seldom between brothers. You say you don't have a brother? That is, when I take a look at you, a great benefit for humankind. Perhaps, in spite of all of the pessimistic prognoses, all is still not lost. But for a man of my age, that problem isn't one of the most pressing ones. "*Après nous, le déluge,*" as Noah said while he was nailing the last planks in his ark. Allow me now to cite the following:

"After the surrender of Austria, several thousand soldiers from the former Austro-Hungarian army returned home with their rifles and ammunition. They grasped the meaning of the word 'freedom' in a strange way. 'If there's freedom, everything's fair game,' they said, and acted accordingly. I remember that it was already the end of January 1919 by the time things got more or less peaceful in Slovakia. I had to leave for Piestany with a reconnaissance battalion to calm things down."

But it would be a mistake if you concluded, on the basis of the citation above, that the idea of loving freedom oh, no was foreign to the Czechs. Oh, no! The Czechs loved freedom, above all their own, just as devotedly as, albeit a bit more cautiously than, the Slovaks did, because if the Slovaks were known for blind courage—the blindness was partly thanks to many years of consuming *dynalkol* and homemade moonshine—then the Czech freedom fighters were rather known as cunning. I could give a thousand examples, but why bother? Why, dear Colonel, carry water to water to the sea? Why give, as instructive as they may be, the sea other examples, comparisons, allegories, and symbols, to delay the moment for which both of us, from the depths of our ardent hearts, are longing? The excitement you may see in me, and which I would try in vain to conceal, does not have its source in fear of crossing the border which in more manner-minded persons would prevent the consummation of the most hidden desires. . . .

"Young friend," the colonel interrupted me, trying almost imperceptibly to reach with his left hand at the switch of the pink lamp, "you're leading me into the temptation to find out with my own eyes what is hidden under fig leaf the fig leaf of your eloquence."

"Dear Colonel," I cried out with fright, which, because the whole room had been plunged into deep darkness, was not at all feigned, "I fear that you'll only discover what is under any other fig leaf, and that you wouldn't be able to avoid the feeling that the result wasn't worth that amount of effort."

At the last words, my voice trembled a little, because I felt how the colonel's feverish palm was gliding along the smooth velvet of my body. . . . What's that? No, he didn't want to iron me, you idiot. His hand simply wandered over my body, something like this, see. . . . No, it didn't wander because it was dark in the room and he couldn't see anything. Why are you sweating so much? If you're so excited by my story, take off your shirt, because then the best is yet to come. Come on, don't be ashamed, you're between men here. What's that? No, actually there's no one else here but the two of us. I meant to say that here you're between a man. So go ahead! Should I help you with the buttons? Your hands are trembling, I see. You can manage by yourself? Glad to hear it. The wasted effort put into your education wasn't entirely in vain after all.

Now, where were we? Oh yes, Slovaks! Some of them made a very profitable business out of their love of freedom. For example, the famous magician Houdini . . . have you heard of him? Slovak to the bone. No, I don't mean that bloody, I mean that healthy. You didn't know that, did you? He had no equal in his field. His most famous number consisted of having his hands and feet locked up, then they sewed him into a sack, locked up like that, and threw the sack into deep water. They didn't even have time to collect the ticket money from everyone who was watching without paying before our dear Houdini was back on the surface, laughing, as free as a bird. . . . And if I may express myself metaphorically, the love of freedom was the life preserver that brought him safely back to the surface. Swim? Certainly he knew how to swim. What, you say it's no great feat then! So you know how to swim too? Would you allow me a rather intimate question: What stroke? The doggy

smooth velvet of my body

Houdini

doggy paddle

paddle, right? That sweet but characteristic detail expressively sketches your profile. All in all, it wasn't even necessary. *Mir reicht's,* or that's enough, as they used to say in similar cases back in the Austro-Hungarian days.

Let's drop it. This has nothing to do with swimming. Swimming isn't an expression of love for freedom, but an ordinary act of self-preservation. Especially the doggy paddle. Any dog would certainly confirm that for you. As for the freedom-loving Houdini—which is understandably a pseudonym; his real last name was Kisfaludi-Močidlanský —one basic detail escaped you: They threw him into the water sewn into a bag, with his hands and feet locked up. And as the ancient Romans used to say, that's the trick.

Have you ever had your hands and feet tied up? Well, so it's high time then. . . . Are you really sure there's nothing left in the bottle? All right then. The shop across the street should still be open. No, no, thank you, you can keep your one hundred drops, you miser. I should have a piece of string around here somewhere. . . . Here it is. You're right, it's mountain-climbing rope. It's just a souvenir from the time when I chased Hazi Schwarzwald Sextett through the Savoy Alps. As the teacher of nations John Amos Comenius used to say, "There's nothing more important than vividness, especially when we want to explain something to children or people with a lower intelligence."

John Amos

Dear young friend, I myself, if I may set aside my proverbial modesty for the moment, I myself in my best years—which still are not, incidentally, so long ago—belonged among the outstanding lovers of freedom, and I would be glad to show you now by hand. Take that little piece of string—well, now, are you listening? then move! —and tie me up. Let's say, feet first, so I couldn't escape. Ha, ha. Just don't hesitate. What, they stink? Don't be a sissy! A man who has decided to knead the soil of history . . . I'm watching you, I'm watching, and slowly everything is beginning to become clear to me. When they

the soil of history

taught how to tie knots at your school, you weren't there, were you? But I guess you know the seaman's knot. What, you served in a tank battalion instead? I see, I see. Dear friend, I'm not the type who is easily driven to despair, but at this moment. . . .

Give it to me! You are, as I can see, left-handed in both hands. For a lack of time and, I should confess, also for a lack of saintly patience on my part—not that saintly patience wouldn't appear in a wide spectrum of my qualities, but I'm afraid that the rest of it has already been used up in this conversation with you—I'll show you only the most basic knots, the so-called knots primer. Don't let the English terms bother you; it's just basic professional terminology, like the Latin terms they use for anatomical designations in medicine. Do you speak English? You don't even have to answer. Where are you living, man? Nowadays, when even in North America every little kid speaks English. . . .

So then: For the feet, people tend to like the so-called constrictor knot. Put your legs together! It's very easy to do, and at the same time, it's relatively reliable. We pull the string from right to left; from your point of view that will naturally be reversed. Try it; see whether it holds! Good. For the hands we should use, we should use . . . but why not, let's use the "jamming hitch"; that suits our purposes perfectly. As the name already indicates, this hitch will jam you up a little. We usually tie the hands behind the back, but in that case you wouldn't be able to watch me, so for pedagogical purposes we'll try it in a frontal position. One, two, three, and all done. A piece of cake. Are you going to remember how to do it? I think you will. You'll see, you're going to remember it until your death.

Have you ever tested your love of freedom? Well, now we have the perfectly suitable conditions for it. In an easy formula, "ró times n over t," where "ró" stands for the diameter of the rope in millimeters, "n" stands for the number of knots, and "t" the time in seconds that you would need to loosen them, you substitute actual quantities and have the result almost immediately. Don't wiggle so much! Can't you feel that you're only pulling the knots tighter? When I look at you, I see that the time "t" should be measured for you in hours, and even so it wouldn't lead anywhere. One thing's for sure, you'll never be a Houdini. You could still play the title role in the film version of the famous fairy tale "The Ugly Duckling." That skinny swan's neck, that beakish nose, and then when you flap your arms around helplessly, just as if you had wings. . . .

Don't quack, don't quack, little duckling. You'd do better to cover yourself with a dignified silence. It'll be better from an aesthetic point of view as well. The view of your sunken chest is, frankly speaking, melancholy. And those slender trembling shoulders . . . I hope you're not crying? Goethe It's a bit too early for that. *Jedem das Seine,* as Goethe said. To each his own. Everything has its time.

Dear son—I hope you'll forgive me for addressing you as such in this moment of truth—dear son, now you see where your thoughtless longing for knowledge has brought you. The path to knowledge must be taken in a differential manner. Not all knowledge is enriching, or, to put it less pathetically, not all knowledge is worth it. What did you gain when you sneaked into my vicinity, seemingly unknown, under the pretext of an interest in one of the oldest professions? I say "seemingly," because one look at the collarbone little hollow beneath your collarbone was enough for me, and if any shadow of doubt had remained with me, that birthmark on your neck—don't move; I don't want to pinch you—would have definitively dismissed it. What kind of liberating truth were you trying to reach? Perhaps you needed to be cured of the deep trauma of your illegitimate origins, you captive of prejudices? Because you wanted to avenge the disgraced honor of your mother, who for everything that is good in her should be grateful to . . . well, can you guess? Not to books, you idiot, to me. Without me she wouldn't have even known how to read, the illiterate ninny. You had, God help us, the thought of embracing me at the end of our meeting, calling out with emotion, in a trembling voice: "Father!"? Brrr. Or did you want to play out the punishing hand of providence? Did you want to delight in the powerlessness of a sinful old man, inebriated by your cheap wine? So delight in it, but quickly, because our ways are parting. Incest makes me sick, and you aren't even my type.

So now I'll leave you to your fate. Soon you'll be convinced that the learning process is not a streetcar that you can step on and off of as you like. But don't take it as a threat. There are some exciting moments ahead of you. You'll broaden your horizons with new experiences, you'll be entertained, you'll learn. . . . And if by chance the process of learning doesn't take the route you assumed it would, don't let yourself be disappointed, because it still applies, dear Colonel. . . . What's that? I know you're a reserve corporal; I'm not talking to *you*. . . . Dear Colonel, it still applies, as Goethe famously said, that gray is theory and ever green is . . .

". . . the horse of life!" the colonel cried out, opening the door on the cabinet, and when he stretched his stiffened limbs, he joyfully neighed.

• • •

Bibliography

The phenomenal mental ability and encyclopedic education of our anonymous author (whose incognito we have preserved, for understandable reasons) is also proved by the fact that in support of the opinions in his narrative, he has unobtrusively and perhaps also unintentionally woven in citations from major works of professional literature.

We remain convinced that knowledge is the property of all the masses, but because copyright law wreaks havoc in the publishing business, we are providing at least those works whose citations we were able to safely identify, as follows:

Bednárik, Rudolf. *Slovenská vlastiveda II* [*Knowledge of Our Slovak Nation II*]. Bratislava, 1943.

Bilý, Klíma. *Strucny pruvodce po Slovensku* [*Brief Guide to Slovakia*]. Šolc and Šimacek.

Cáp, J., and Dytrych, Z. *Utvárení osobnosti v nárocnych zivotních situacích* [*Personality Formation under Demanding Circumstances*]. Státní pedagogické nakladelství, 1968.

Collective. *Dermatovenerologie* [*Dermatovenerology*]. Státní zdravotnické nakladelství, 1965.

Collective. *Slovensko 2, Príroda* [*Slovakia 2, Nature*]. Obzor, 1972.

Handbuch für Donaureisen [*Tour Guide for Travel along the Danube*]. Verlag Payer u. Cowlen, 1936.

Hynie, Prof. MU Dr. Josef, Dr.Sc. *Lekárska sexuológia* [*Medical Sexology*]. Osveta, 1970.

Matiášek, Bárta, Soukup. *Vyslech a psychologie* [*Interrogation and Psychology*]. Orbis, 1966.

Matiášek, Soukup, Bárta. *Psychologie a vyslechová praxe* [*Psychology and Interrogation Practice*]. Orbis, 1968.

Pardel, Tomás. *Problémy psychoanalytického hnutia* [*Problems of the Psychoanalytic Movement*]. Unpublished psychodiagnosis, 1972.

Pondelícek, Ivo, and Pondelícková-Mašlová, Jaroslava. *Lidská sexualita* [*Human Sexuality*]. Avecenum, 1971.

Praha prírodovedecká, lékarská a technická, Odborny pruvodce k VI. sjezdu ceskoslov. prírodozptycu, lékaru a inzenýru [*Scientific, Medical, and Technical Prague: Proceedings of the 6th Congress of Czechoslovak Scientists, Physicians, and Engineers*]. Prague, 1928.

Rybár, Dr. Ján. *Sociálnopsychologické úvahy o povahe reci a jej zivote* [*Social-Psychological Considerations on the Function of Language and Its Life*]. Self-published, Nové Mesto nad Váhom, 1944.

Servít, Zdenek. *Nervové záchvaty* [*Neurological Seizures*]. Nakladatelství CSAV, 1960.

Turciansky Svāty Martin a okolie [*Turciansky Svāty Martin and Its Surroundings*]. Published by the local branch of Matica Slovenska.

Zimák, Jozef, ed. *Vpád madarskych bolševikov na Slovensko v roku 1919* [*The 1919 Invasion of Slovakia by the Hungarian Bolsheviks*].

■ □ ■ □ ■

A HORSE UPSTAIRS,
A BLIND MAN IN VRÁBLE

In memory of Katerina Josefa Obernauerová
(1905–1956)

1

> "Men," said Xenophone, "received from the gods
> the gift of teaching other men with words, so
> that they will know what they should do. We
> cannot teach a horse with words."

Before turning onto the main road, the bus stopped for a
moment to give the right of way. "I had such funny night-
mares," she said. All the sangfroid, all the cynicism in the
world can't keep us from thinking that life has a logical
construction, something like a staircase, or rather, like an
eye-pleasing roundness. Get thee to a university, Ophelia!

We could come up with a sentence on any subject—a
bus, life, or perhaps the little town of Vráble. We could say
of Vráble, for example: town of 4,200 inhabitants, altitude
142 meters. Post office, train station, bus station. Vestiges
of Neolithic times and the Bronze Age; an *oppidum* from
Roman and barbarian times. The first recorded mention of
the town was in 1265. By 1294, it was already an important
market town; in the sixteenth century, the town was sacked
by the Turks; in the seventeenth century, thanks to the rapid
development in trade, it became a major postal center. And

The epigraphs to the numbered chapters are taken from the book *The Rider
and His Horse,* by Lieutenant Colonel Bruno Jaksch (Hodonin, 1927).

so on to the present: Lodging, Tourist Hotel "Žitavan," two stars, 6 Main Street, tel. 22-37. . . . There's nothing remarkable about these phrases, but they suffice.

One day in London, a young woman who knew me slightly and who, because of my contacts with a number of older men, thought that I might have some problems of sexual orientation (this post-Freudian and pop psychology is widespread in the West). . . . We could come up with a sentence on any subject, but to create a simple sentence about oneself is difficult.

Let's start over. One day, a young woman, a certain Beverley. It's been so many years now, and the things she reminds me of! Beverley was not pretty. Under her halo of blond hair, she had a swollen face, like a peasant in her ninth month of pregnancy; she wasn't pretty, but she shone. A ball of avidity, of interior heat. . . . But what good is it to speak of an interior, since we know that beyond a certain depth, other persons are nothing but our own mental construction? Maybe that's why we cling so much to everything superficial; we stick to it, comforted, because that's where a man is himself, where he differs from the rest. Beverley was upset that her black students in New Orleans had refused to read Shakespeare because he wasn't black. Apparently, with his totally different experience, he had nothing to say to them. The greatest dramatist for them was LeRoi Jones. I laughed: LeRoi Jones is black, it's true, but he's certainly no Shakespeare. If I had to make a choice between the two, I don't know if I would have leaned toward their choice. I was aware of the ridiculousness of their behavior, but at the same time, I could identify with them. They were on the right path, although clearly just at the beginning. When they reached the end, perhaps they'd have some surprises. I don't read Shakespeare either: he wasn't me.

That day, on the evening of her departure, Beverley drank a little too much gin, and when she went out on the balcony, I followed her because I was afraid she might be sick. Night was falling softly and in the park across from us, a bronze Gandhi sitting cross-legged on his pedestal had turned his back to us. . . .

Let's go back to our story, for the second time: One day, a young woman asked me: "Do you love your mother?" In English, the word "love" has become so banal; in English, you can love pizza, rock and roll, and even Beckett, although people like me still feel a certain embarrassment . . . but all things considered, it wasn't the only reason; I really meant it, because if you have to answer such a question, as naive as it is touching, you can only answer sincerely . . . and I really meant it when I said: "I don't know, I've never done anything for her yet. She's never really needed me, so how could I be sure?"

2

Right at the beginning of the first lesson, we
should begin to impose our will on the horse.
We should always do the opposite of what
the horse wants.

I'm losing my patience with these complete sentences, without any interruption, with this style of narration dispatched like a train from the depot.

"You can't say a thing like that to me anymore," I told my wife yesterday at the station.

"I don't understand why I can't say that the trains have been awfully dirty recently. I must be an idiot, but you have to explain it to me."

"Another one of these imprecisions," I said calmly, because I really didn't want to fight. There was really no need for her to take out her handkerchief at that very moment and wipe the metal trim of the window before resting her elbows there, but that itself was rather funny too. "You can tell your boss or your friend Betka whatever you want to. All I'm saying is that you shouldn't tell me things like that. What do you really want to say? What does 'recently' mean? Last year, the last two months, today, or just since five o'clock in the afternoon? And then, do you come regularly to the station to check the trains? If I remember correctly, you haven't taken the train for six months, or more. And then, perhaps you mean that there's some dirt in your compartment? You still need to be more precise: Is there some vomit? Or some pieces of paper around? Or maybe . . ."

"Be patient," she said with a resignation that, had it been sincere, might have been taken for wise sadness; I like it when she acts like that, and sometimes I suspect she's aware of this. "The train leaves in two minutes and you'll be rid of us for a while."

"Five minutes!"

"Well, then, five minutes. But you see, you've understood very well what I meant. I don't really know why I have to take an hour to think over every word I say."

"Because you're leaving the same disorder behind as that cleaning service," I said, but she wasn't listening to me anymore. "Come and say good-bye to Dad," she told our daughter, who was reading a magazine at the end of the compartment, "even if he doesn't deserve it." I'm happy that my daughter, with her nimble spirit, refuses the static character of routine good-byes, that standing yourself up on sentimental tiptoes, and that she prefers to read, even if I'm not crazy about her choice of reading material. "Kiss-kiss!" she said, and went back to the end of the compartment. "Oh!" sighed my wife, a little disconcerted, because suddenly she didn't know which of us to attack. The soul of this family! All three of us, separately, were quite tolerable people, but as a family we were unbearable.

The whistle brutally terminated this round; the buffers creaked and I was already going down the stairs; I didn't turn back but I knew that if I did, I would see my wife in the window, and that her lurking hand, already on the lookout, would have started to wave. How easy it is to be nasty when we're sure of always having someone, in the backdrop, to make a contrast with ourselves. But when all the roles of good guys are already taken, what else can we do, if we want to keep at least a semblance of individuality?

On the way home, I thought about my daughter and her funny way of saying good-bye. My daughter's behavior most often aroused ambivalent feelings in me—there were things about her that I liked, and others that I strongly disliked. For example, several days earlier, she had come, completely upset, to tell me: "Today, on the Market Square, I saw a girl jump out of the window. It was in the corner building, the one where the pharmacy is." I had to say something, I knew, but as usual, the first thing to come out was a stupid parental reaction: "And what were you doing down there?"

"I was on the bus. And suddenly I saw it, it was as if someone had thrown a coat out of the window, I saw her fall, totally limp. From the fourth floor. By the time I got there, she was already dead."

I was on guard. The comparison with the coat had attracted my attention—not because of its precision, I couldn't judge that, but because she had shown a certain sense of observation. But the fact that she got off the bus, took the underground passageway, running . . . to be an onlooker like that, excited, with bulging eyes. . . . It's true that at her age, these things were happening to her for the first time, so it was no surprise that she had wanted to witness it.

"She did it because of an unhappy love," she said with awe, but a strangely jubilant one, as if she had just met a fairy.

"And how do you know that, young lady?"

"That's what they were saying around there; there were people from the apartment building. They knew all about it. She fell in love with some boy and was unhappy."

I dropped it. Be that as it may, I hadn't been there, and she had. In any case, it was only the path of least resistance:

casting doubt on the information, when what is needed is to cast doubt on the event itself.

"Well, you see," I said, "if she had waited a little while, it would have passed, and she could have had plenty of other unhappy loves. And then, what's this attribution of positive signs and negative signs, like in math, happy love, unhappy love? What kind of attitude is that? Is it a matter of choice: I only want a happy love, I won't accept an unhappy one? And if it starts to go a little badly, I'll just jump out the window?" It didn't matter to me if my daughter was going to detest me for these words, because to me, being detestable was one of the duties of a parent. I was only afraid I was shooting off-target.

"But really," I said, "what did she want to say by all that? What did she really want to show by that? Don't tell me . . . okay, she wanted to kill herself . . . but don't tell me that if somebody jumps like that, in the middle of the day, on a square, from the fourth floor . . . you surely must feel that . . . there's some kind of gesture behind all this; she wanted to say something. But what? That her unhappy love was as big as a four-story building? And that if it had been even bigger, even unhappier, she would have jumped from the sixth story? Or maybe she just wanted to say that her love was the kind that makes you jump out the window? In that case, it would have been enough for her to have jumped out the window on the ground floor!"

I actually would have liked that kind of despair, sincere but capable of self-derision, but I didn't say that. I had no doubt that problems in one's love life couldn't be solved by jumping out of a window, and I would have even considered it my duty, for the sake of prevention, to make such an act as repugnant to my daughter as possible, but yet . . . all the time I felt that there was a superior, universal sense in that absurd, infantile, and hysterical act: the girl, by jumping, had bequeathed us the absolute measure of love, which we could admire just as you might admire the standard meter in Paris. It has no use for anyone in everyday life either, but we all know that it exists.

"She lived there, on the fourth floor, that's why," my daughter said. And bam!

Get thee to a university, Ophelia! I said to myself in desperation. In any case, the only thing that attracts you in this whole event is the misleading image seen in some bad film: you floating on the surface of a stream, surrounded by flowers, your dress spread out. . . . Or perhaps you want your love to be discussed in the papers? Well, read this: "With the heat wave, accidents are once again our top story. The main cause of this: People are careless and overestimate their strength. Yesterday, in River X, near Village Y, a body was recovered and identified as O.P., age 19, who had been walking along the steep bank when she unfortunately slipped into the water and was carried away by the current. A single careless moment, and the water had claimed another victim."

Get thee to a university, Ophelia! But what if we saw her again, forty years later, as a concierge, in a sweatsuit and an apron with a flowery design. Look, there she is, standing on the sidewalk and talking with the neighbor who's taking her doggie for a walk (a Pekingese, I might mention in passing): "And on Wednesday the butcher was out of bacon again. What do you say to that?" Has this long-forgotten tragedy been made any less tragic by the fact that she herself no longer understood it?

3

> The horse is not a very intelligent animal.
> We cannot take its rare marks of intelligence as
> mental activity; they're only its natural instincts.

Recently I've started to get up at night and turn on the lamp in order to look at myself. No, that's not exactly it;

I've been getting up in the hope that perhaps at night, by unexpectedly turning on the lamp, I would surprise, like stupefied cockroaches, the leftovers of myself: namely, those parts of my being that have no practical application and are of no interest to anyone else. . . . I certainly don't seem to be explaining myself very well. But that's just a side issue. In short, let's say it like this: my own private Self. I'm not thinking of anything grandiose; I'd be satisfied with a single phrase firm enough to stand on its own two feet, and even jump a little, like we sometimes do on a pure whim, when no one in the street is watching.

But there was nothing. Out of that, I mean out of that emptiness, ensue certain eccentricities and acts that appear absurd, my own private Galileo: "I do move, though." "I don't see any other explanation for it. The other day, for example, I went to the State Pension Office. Why there exactly, you might ask; perhaps just because it was on my way. Of course, a grown man needs a justification for everything he does, and in this case, it was a timid hope: What if I succeed? So I went to the State Pension Office, I found a door and behind it a pleasant gentleman with white hair—but it wasn't God, because he lacked the beard, and the skin of the top of his head, visible under his sparse hair, was a disarming pink—and I said: "I propose assumption instead of aging."

It could be that I didn't use those exact words; maybe I presented my proposition in the form of a question: "Would it be possible to have an assumption instead of aging?" But it doesn't really matter. I was expecting him to send me to the Departmental Institute of Public Health, at the Ministry of Health, or that he'd at least ask me: "Last name, first name, date of birth?" But the man just looked at me without being surprised, even with a certain admiration, as a sign of respect for what I had just asked, as if I had been an upstart to find an answer all by myself that had taken the administration months, if not years, to elaborate, and he answered me: "It's already been taken care of."

And wham! I had already reflected on certain details (for example, an annual checkup after one turns sixty, or perhaps a Rorschach test to diagnose the feeling of life—in place of ink spots they could use a map of Central Europe with its constantly changing borders), but there, what could you add? "There it is." He wrapped these words in a paper bag of a smile, gave them back to me, and that was it. I would have liked to ask him what heaven was like; was it an eco-museum? And then, how easily he accepted my terminology! As if we had explained everything to each other in advance.

I don't know what I was waiting for, but when I turned into our street—I still call it that, although I haven't lived there for a long time—and I saw a black flag at half-mast on the apartment building, I wasn't surprised at all. "It's already been taken care of." Indeed, what could I think? While waiting for the elevator, I learned from my fourth-floor neighbor that Plačkova had died.

That was another time. This time, I told myself: "You haven't taken a trip for a long while and here's your chance," and I decided to take a bus trip. The bus was obviously a way out, but a grown man needs an excuse for everything he does. For this trip, I decided to fall in love with a town called Vráble. Why Vráble, of all places? Because a girl whom we can call, for no specific reason, Miss Laktišová, passed through there or found herself there by chance sometime. It's a petty reason that doesn't tell you much about Vráble, but perhaps it says something about my relationship with Miss Laktišová. I was, let's say, in the mood for Laktišová.

When all is said and done, I told myself, who cares that my reason is petty? The pettier the better. Because that way, there was more room left for me.

Where is the center of gravity in the horse? In
a nonharnessed and immobile horse, it's located
almost exactly at the horse's heart.

I had a sleepless night. The bus was leaving very early, and
so I woke up several times as a precaution. What's more, in
the early morning I had my recurrent dream. (I should
mention that I don't attach any significance to dreams, but
they do leave their mark on one's conscience.) I dream that
behind the first Bratislava is a second, totally different one.
I go for walks there. Nothing ever happens to me, I don't
meet anyone, I just walk around, and I'm happy. Behind
the castle and the cathedral extends a large square, then hills
with enormous oak trees whose branches let sunbeams
shine through them. You can also get there by the road that
leads toward the port. That's where the second Bratislava
begins. Suddenly, as if behind an unfamiliar door, a city
opens up, a city that we've wanted, an animated city, ocher
in color. How easy it is to be happy, at least in a dream. It's
always very short, but every time I have enough time to tell
myself: Finally, back home.

The second Bratislava doesn't exist, and it never existed,
of course. But sometimes, while awake, I'm able to perceive
it for a fraction of a second, something like its not-quite-
faithful portrait. A snapshot. A quick bite in the neck.

This dream of Bratislava isn't new, but for forty years it's
been part of my basic repertoire. At the beginning, I
explained it as an illusion of déjà vu. Now I know that it
isn't new; it's been part of my basic repertoire for forty years.
Or rather, something seen in advance, perhaps. It's my
homeland that appears to me in dreams, and when I wake
up, I realize that in this world, there is no homeland. In this
way, death becomes familiar; it reconciles me to the idea
that I'm only here on a visit and that at the end, I'll go
home. There's no place like home.

A HORSE UPSTAIRS, A BLIND MAN IN VRÁBLE

> All teaching and breaking-in destined to gain the
> trust and the obedience of the horse must take
> place before feeding, so that the oats appear to
> the horse as a reward.

At four o'clock, when morning was approaching, the cat scratched at the door. She had already slept enough and probably thought I had already slept enough too. She was wrong. Oh, well. I opened the door because I knew that I was the weaker one; we had already figured that out. There was a time when I wanted to educate my cat, to inculcate the idea in her that man is the master of nature, but she eventually proved me wrong.

I've known a number of cats in my life, and I don't delude myself about my own cat; I know that she has big ears, a rather narrow head, and a stomach that hangs down from lack of exercise. I also know that the adjective "my," which I'm using here, is, contrary to the rules of grammar, demonstrative and not possessive. Of course, there are people who say "my cat" and think that way too, but in doing that, they only show their blindness to reality.

The cat jumped on my bed. She scolded me for having made her wait, all the while waddling around on me as if she wanted to dig a litterbox in my rib cage. But that was only for show. Immediately afterward, she gave me one or two nudges on the chest with her cold and damp nose. This was also just for play. She didn't even wait for my reaction before leaving to be bored somewhere else. A half hour later, while waking up, I saw her sitting in the middle of the room, pensively watching my bed.

(Every time I see a cat, this time for example, with her head lightly tilted and her tail curled around her paws, I feel pleasure, a sort of aesthetic appeal; this is where the interpretation and appropriation begin, from which we create our own image of the cat. It could be that this was the determining factor for the domestication of animals. Man chose those that most appealed to his senses, that most satisfied his obscure but pressing aesthetic feelings . . . or perhaps it's the opposite, and those criteria that allow us to perceive the relative beauty of an aesthetically indifferent being arose only at the end of long years of living together? But that's irrelevant. The important thing is knowing whether we pay them in return with our own elegance, our charm. It is this question that haunts me when, early in the morning, by chance, I open my eyes: What if, behind this apparently absent look, behind these yellow pupils, nothing was hidden but disgust? In those moments, I try to guess what she sees. A sleeper, especially seen from below, draws attention to himself with his fragility, emphasized by his open mouth and his nostrils, so large and vulgar: the fragility of the idiot. He sleeps curled up, his duvet pulled up to his yellowish ear, which he never moves. Not once!)

Well, yes, if I wanted to include the cat in my world, I had to resort to this sort of anthropomorphic interpretation. In the past, I flattered myself that I had a cat who waited for me ("with a mute animal devotion"). I even claimed to feel her impatient call in the air: "So wake up already." These days, when she's following me, meowing, to the bathroom, like now, I just tell myself that she would do the same for anyone, very happy to see something move, to have a bit of a distraction. You can see that I've become more modest, which doesn't mean that I'm any closer to the truth. The advantage of a cat is that she doesn't try to refute our false conjectures. When all is said and done, she also knows me like the back of her paw, and finds a feline explanation for all of my gestures. It would be hard for me to surprise her, unless perhaps by suddenly bursting into tears, for example, because she's never seen that before. In short, we don't contradict each other, we don't disturb our respective prejudice. You could say that we have found a modus vivendi.

The cat's meowing intensified as I approached the kitchen. At times she howled as if someone had stepped on her paw. Then she got ahead of me and lured me toward the kitchen. "You greedy pig!" I insulted her loudly, because I didn't have to worry about waking anyone up in the empty apartment. "You disgusting creature!" The cat knows that this was only an attempt to conceal my capitulation, so she wasn't even offended. Suddenly silent, she watched me open the refrigerator and take out a beef lung, then she jumped on the table, walked with confidence between the plates and the glasses, glanced into the sink, and grabbed a piece of meat out of it with her paw. "Get down!" I said in vain, because the cat was ignoring me royally, and when I finally pushed her to the floor, she just growled and jumped right back up. Yes, maybe she's a creature with base instincts, but she's free. I realized that the cat was on a much higher level than me, but since the category of freedom seemed a little too complicated for me, I found a completely simple physical explanation for her superiority: a cat always lands on her feet. No, you can't say that she doesn't know how to curl herself around your feet, that she doesn't know how to beg for a piece of meat or a petting, that she never takes a refusal and doesn't accept any compromise. She's just not affected by it. For her, each time is simply an isolated event, an accident without consequences. She immediately regains her dignity, endures my attempts at affection, moves her ears to make me understand that two's a crowd, and when that's not enough, she yawns, pulling back her jaw, and goes to sit down somewhere else. But when she wants to warm up her belly from my body heat, she comes over to my armchair without any scruples, watches me a moment as if I were prey, then jumps, crying out "Here I am!" onto my knees. Only humans are paralyzed by memory. You can also say it this way: The cat has no ideas about herself and thus can never be in conflict with them. And therein rests the elementary freedom of the cat.

After I finished washing, shaving, and combing myself, and after I gave the cat something to eat, I could finally leave for the bus station. "Bye now!" I called out politely from the door. "See you tonight!" No answer, of course. Sometimes she calls out to me when I walk past her, even seven times in a row, but other times. . . . So much for the cat.

6

In general, one can keep to the following principle: The horse should be short in height and broad in width. It should occupy a large surface space. The Germans say: *Das Pferd muss auf viel Boden stehen.* "The horse covers a lot of sunshine!"

As for the horse . . . just a few words: A child is always ready to be amazed; it lets itself be amazed by anything. It isn't astonished; it's amazed. Astonishment assumes some logical objection, a violated precondition; amazement accepts things without any conditions. The stupefying thing about seeing a horse close up is the size, and the staircase suddenly looked tiny.

I should note that at the time, a horse in itself was not something rare, even for city children. We all knew the blue wagon of the post office, which transported parcels. In the front, the coachman's seat with the wheel-crank for the brake, and in the back, an opening with bars and a step onto which one could jump while the wagon was moving. This wagon was pulled by a horse. When it stopped in front of our house, we would come up to it and stroke the white star on its forehead. We weren't even afraid. It was, it's true, a rather special horse, a civil-servant horse.

7

If you have the opportunity, and if the environment allows you to go out into the countryside,

taking a two- or three-hour tour, twice a week,
is highly beneficial at this time.

Finally I'm on board the bus. Everyone has been on a bus before. This one is headed for a spa town, and for this reason waiting in front of the door you see ladies of a certain age, with freshly permed hair and enormous suitcases. There's also a man in a navy-blue suit with a big black briefcase. There are other people, and if I really wanted to forget about my problems, I would just have to devote all of my attention to the passengers and observe them for hours, but I haven't reached that point of desperation. In fact, among all the passengers just one had attracted my attention—a man with black hair and a graying beard, reading a newspaper. That's what intrigued me about him: How could a man who has invested in himself enough to let his beard grow read on a bus? And a newspaper at that! Had he run out of curiosity, had he lost all hope?

It seemed to me that I knew him from somewhere; I was sure that if he shaved off his beard, I'd find him to be a classmate from sixth grade or a friend from military service. Those red cheeks, which exuded health, and those thick eyebrows. . . .

"Reading newspapers is the mass tourism of the spirit!" I amicably reprimanded the man *in petto*. I decided that we had known each other during military service: among war veterans, comrades in arms, this rough frankness is entirely permissible.

The man was reading the first page, and if I leaned forward a bit, I could read over his shoulder.

"It must be stated openly that wheat has become, in the historical frame of the class struggle between socialism and capitalism, a universal weapon of strategic impact, where imperialism, notably American imperialism, temporarily occupies a position of strength toward the socialist countries."

A single sentence, a half-open window, and the fresh breeze of the social problem came into the bus. Well, yes, when you're in a mess of your own, there's no better distraction than a little social problem. Nothing improves your morale like knowing you're not the only one with problems.

"The reality of the past year should have been a sufficient lesson for all of the workers of the management sector, but above all, for all of the committees and members of the cells of the Slovak Communist Party in the agricultural enterprises, who should have taken concrete measures to improve the quality of the ensilage, as well as its daily and intensive control. The past year, that is, the downgrading of more than 37 percent of fodder in the third and fourth quality categories should never be repeated."

If we want these words to make sense, we must be able to imagine something behind the words. Perhaps not everyone, but at least that's the case for me. It's probably a personal fault to react to the aggression of language with the aggression of my imagination. The process takes place unconsciously, beginning with an intuitive feeling of the connections between words. In this paragraph which, furthermore, doesn't leave much room for imagination, I understood that it was attacking last year's events. Last year, that bitch! I thought, and then she sprang up before my eyes: bleached blond hair, a provocative smile on her outrageously parted lips, loose, flabby tights. And that raucous voice—how vulgar! As if she had two glasses of beer in her throat in place of vocal cords. Still a minor, and what shamelessness! How had she been able to infiltrate among us, our group of decent people?

"One cannot call this anything but wastage and thus, in a certain sense, treason on the grain front: the fact that the farmers had not used corn as ensiled fodder, when it is known that the dry fibrous stem of the corn contains 50 percent calories more than the straw of grains."

I had already started to resist, but it was useless: it's dangerous to expose yourself to language. At the beginning, she was nothing but a long black skirt with some dirty boots sticking out beneath it, but then she emerged from under her checked scarf, with two large canines in a gaping mouth: "treason on th grain front." A wart at the tip of the nose, a gray, peeling mustache on the upper lip. Satisfied, she rubbed together her gnarled hands, covered with freckles. I was a little ashamed of the banal drift of my imagination: in the malevolent saboteur, I recognized the old owner of the gingerbread house, force-feeder of children. But why was she all alone in this deserted field, why was she bent over, breathing on the embers of a tiny fire? Oh, perfidious betrayer of my people!

"The heavy artillery on the grain front, in point of view of the cattle breeders, is no doubt, in predominantly grain-producing regions, the corn which, produced in the Transcarpathian process and calling on the complex mechanism of the Soviet machinery complex and scientific agrotechnology, never yields less than eight tons of grain per hectare."

That sentence had caught my imagination with the phrase "Transcarpathian process," and I pictured a sturdy muzhik, slightly obese, in linen pants and fur cap, with a bushy handlebar mustache. It was very brief, an outline rather than a portrait, an image that didn't take definite shape, because I felt sick and turned my head away.

8

> The English have reached the point of claiming that the equestrian "art" is superfluous and that it's quite enough that the rider and the horse understand where they want to go.

The bus went onto the highway and, to my left, in that clear summer day, the mountains were brutally detaching themselves at the bottom of the sky because of their dark green shadow. All at once I realized, perhaps for the first time in my life, that the sky was part of nature. Is it possible? So much beauty! And free for all the world to take!

"Killing time, when it's really a question of living it to the fullest!" I said to the bearded man, in a reproachful tone. I really like to spill out that kind of half-truth, even if, as at that moment, I know you have to kill time once in a while, so that living it has some meaning.

"I love these enthusiasts," the bearded man said without turning, because he had also noticed me and probably recognized me. "Sunday geniuses. But, old man, I take this bus almost every day."

"Good for you!" I retaliated, to show him that he couldn't beat me so easily. "So you have the opportunity to appreciate the fine nuances."

I succeeded in making the bearded man laugh; it had already come to that. He had a raucous laugh that came loose from his throat in little balls.

"But still," he said after having spat out the last one, "how does it happen that I run into you on a bus? If memory serves me correctly, back in the military service you always hitchhiked home."

"In those days, I had plenty of time and not much money. These days, it's the opposite. These days I would hitchhike only if somebody stole my wallet or I missed my last connection."

"You think that would be worth it?" the bearded man asked. "I mean, stealing your wallet."

"I can't really say," I said, and tried to mentally count the money I had on me. It was certain that it wouldn't be a sin, just a breach of the code of socialist life.

"And you, Brutus, do you have a bank card by now too?" he asked.

"No, not yet. I'm still resisting. It's my one shining point, a little victory for myself, a provisory one, of course, in the irresistible process of rampant banalization and progressive depreciation. And what about you, doesn't that just kill you? It's enough to think that every minute—tell me a number, something high: ten thousand?—that every minute, ten thousand children come into this world, and thus every minute, you're ten thousand times less important. All right, nobody can do anything, I know, but you're above all that, you're reading a newspaper on the bus!"

"It's pure demagoguery," he said, releasing more balls of laughter, of glass wool. "I could answer you that at the same time, every minute, I don't know how many people are dying, six thousand or something, and so every minute you're six thousand times more important. But it's not a question of that. Because there's a sort of phenomenon, let's call it, for example, the life cycle in nature, and every person who's concerned with concrete, palpable things, everyone except maybe a few completely marginal literary types . . . but I don't want to insult you: Are you still interested in literature?"

"Literature," I said, "is every bit as concrete as egg salad or a cow's udder. They sell it, in case you didn't know, in bookstores."

"It's just that egg salad and cows' udders have a purpose. But as for literature . . ."

"I'll give you an example in response. I hope that your neighbor . . ."

(I don't know why—perhaps it's an unconscious way of settling oneself in a new context: we're thinking of something else, but at the same time we're feeling the objects that surround us, we give them a name and a place—I don't know why, but I had come to the conclusion that the woman seated next to my bearded friend was his girlfriend. Perhaps because when she arrived, she had hung up her jacket next to the window, leaned her head on it, and dozed off. In reality, she couldn't have fallen asleep so quickly, she was just pretending, but just because of that game. . . . A wife, disillusioned by frequent trips with her husband, would have fallen asleep like that, but beforehand, even with her eyes closed, she would lavish him with absurd orders: not to forget to buy grass seed in Nitra, to watch that his bag didn't turn over, because the tea's in there; half asleep, she would still have the energy to share her questionable observations: that Magda's new hairdo was horrible, that last night she saw a completely wrecked car in town, and then she would complain, more than once, of how hard it was to fall asleep on the bus. I'm not making an attack here on wives in general; this is simply how this specific relation shows itself: by offering the space, the fertile ground, for this spiritual flatulence. Certainly, certainly, he could have had a deaf-mute wife, or perhaps that woman was next to him by chance; but this way of pressing against him with her shoulder—lightly, with respect, as if they weren't touching except with the heat of their skins—that vicious chastity . . . she was impatient: she could go to bed with him anytime, but sleeping next to him was rather rare. That's why I considered her a girlfriend. So thus I was hoping for the opposite of what I was in the middle of saying.)

". . . that your neighbor won't listen to us. I read it in an American journal, *Saturday Review*, but that isn't important. So in America (which, as you well know, is a crazy country), when the feminist movement was at its height, they formed a circle, or association, where jilted women would meet. They would gossip, exchange experiences, and give each other advice on how to manage alone, by themselves, how to survive without men. One day, for example, they learned, under the surveillance of an expert, how to insert a pessary. The question arises, of course, what good would a pessary do them without men, but we'll leave that aside for the moment. The journalist who wrote about this self-taught vocational group liked that course very much, and she particularly stressed that the women had profited from the occasion to compliment each other on their pussies. It seemed that this had reassured them. When all's said and done, I like it too; it's

A HORSE UPSTAIRS, A BLIND MAN IN VRÁBLE

133

touching, in a way; but why am I telling you this? It seems, of course, more natural for a man to reassure a woman on the quality of her sex, and not exactly with words. But in the given situation, this solution imposed itself by default. Well, literature does the same thing. It seeks to convince humanity, that frustrated yet still rather vain woman, that despite everything, she still has a beautiful little pussy. And it's life itself, as they say, which should prove it, and for part of humanity it's probably the case; those people don't need literature. But the others, for lack of more tangible proofs, are reduced to literature.

9

> Give the horse your warmest, kindest look, with
> the friendliest smile possible, then give it an
> angry and irritated look, glare at it furiously, bare
> your teeth; you'll never see the slightest reaction.

"Look, those are . . . ," the bearded man said—I could have guessed he would want to have the last word in front of his girlfriend. "Maybe we didn't understand each other very well, the victory of good over evil and so on; look, those are fairy tales. I was thinking of this—what's it called—realistic literature, only in a respectful tone. For adults. How Tolstoy's Pierre Bezukhov founds a collective farm, or the worries of Madame Bovary during her divorce proceedings. What good is all that?"

"That's very simplistic . . . 'what good is it.' Because people . . . no, I'll give you another example—this is a real event, by the way; I'm not making anything up. One time in England, during a search for a sex killer, the police were looking through a forest where lovers would meet, and purely by chance, they came across a guy sitting in a tree who was watching the couples with binoculars and describing everything he saw to a friend who was sitting underneath the tree, in a wheelchair, masturbating."

"That's what I call a life-and-death friendship," said the bearded man in a provocative tone. Perhaps he just wanted to distract me.

"So that's more or less the situation. Now think about it. This man underneath the tree didn't see anything; he had to imagine the whole scene. Wouldn't it have been more comfortable to imagine the same thing in bed, at home? Yet he had dragged himself out into the forest, in a wheelchair, mind you (and here we've reached the heart of the matter), because at home he knew they were just his own fantasies, but under the tree, listening to his friend with the binoculars—who, we might add in passing, could very well have been telling him tall tales, because how would he have been able to check up on him from down there?—he was able to think that all those fantasies, which, I emphasize, he was imagining by himself, seemed more real to him. . . . Authentic, that's what they call this particular illusion. And it is precisely this illusion, this service . . ."

"You haven't forgotten, I hope, that we're speaking about a cripple."

"And what about you?" I retorted, exasperated. "Would you have been a cripple yourself? Because you, to be concrete, as you say yourself, you're riding a bus, but tell me, are you really riding a bus? You're reading the paper, you're arguing with me about all sorts of nonsense, and then you ask yourself, during this time, what your neighbor, who is right here, would say to this. What? You haven't really ridden a bus until the day you read about the bus trip in *Madame Bovary*."

"You're thinking of the famous scene where she's in the bus to go to her divorce trial?" He found nothing more to add.

10

> It's impossible for a horse, as good as it may be, to be a racehorse, hunting horse, and thorough-bred all at the same time.

A HORSE UPSTAIRS, A BLIND MAN IN VRÁBLE

Desperate times call for desperate measures, I told myself. I'll teach you to kick a man when he's down! Indeed, why is it that these days the first braggart who comes along feels like he can spout off on literature?

I was getting upset in that way for another moment, but at the same time . . . at the word "braggart," I felt that I was grasping the situation poorly: the bearded man was speaking with a certain private bitterness, with a thorn in his tongue, so to speak . . . but at the same time, a terrible suspicion was awakened in me. Was I going to remember, for God's sake, what he had studied? Wasn't it he, or was I dreaming, who had given us lectures in the barracks on the socialist aesthetic of cinematography? Wasn't it he who tried to win points from the officers by trying to recite his own poetry in the Army Creativity Competition? Wasn't it he who had the intention, once having finished his military service, of making a debut in some journal, just to see his name in print? And wasn't it he, by chance, to whom, notwithstanding his sharp poetic colic, or rather in fact because of it, to whom they had given the agricultural column? It was certainly just a hypothesis—the article was an editorial and thus had no signature—but for the moment, provisionally, I believed that those phrases peppered with strategical-tactical metaphors had been written by him.

And there was another one of those guys who had found a cozy nest and now, frustrated, feels nostalgia for the open fields of life. I already know someone like that. The bearded man, at least, comes up with his own sentences, even if they're idiotic, while after years of equivocations, I can only polish and pilfer sentences written by other people. The grapes were sour, weren't they, you bearded fox? I thought, but without anger—strangely enough, it was only now that I began to really like him. I even reached the point of regretting that I had treated him that way, reducing him to his beard. Because the beard . . . yes, why not, but if I had to name something else, a less obvious, less striking trait, irrelevant perhaps, but seen with my own eyes, something that would make that man materialize before me, I couldn't come up with anything. Perhaps the dandruff on his royal-blue collar?

Frustrated nesters of the world, unite!

11

> The horse never stops looking for a way to escape the hold of the reins: in contrast, the rider can't always concentrate his ideas, for hours, on the same thing.

Meanwhile, the bus rolls on, and as the morning comes to life, it is passed, from time to time, by a black Tatra, a gray Volga, or even by a marine-blue Alfa Romeo, registered in Vienna. Those are invented cars, and the big truck rolling painfully in the opposite direction, loaded to the brim with cartons of sugar cubes, is invented too. Perhaps it isn't worth the trouble of talking about them, but I'll say it, in case: This has never happened, not to me, anyway; it is happening, if at all, at this very moment, and to you.

Sládkovičovo is not invented; first of all—but this could still be a mirage—the bluish roof of the castle, like a stamp stuck sideways, appears above the forest, then the bus turns and when the dust that it raised falls back to the ground, everyone can see: it exists.

One can say this about Sládkovičovo: The town is located in the Danube plain, in the Dudvah and Čierna Voda valley; traces of habitation in the Neolithic era, a necropolis (for burial in a curled position) from the Kosihy-Caha civilization, a tumulus dating from the Middle Bronze Age, the remnants of a Germanic village and cremation tombs from the first or second century A.D., Hungarian graves from the tenth century. The district is mentioned for the first time in 1326. In the fourteenth century, it belonged to the Dudvagy family, in the fifteenth century to the Dudvaszeghi family, and in the sixteenth to the Clarist Order of Bratislava. Since the nineteenth century, the town had enjoyed the privilege of having a market. In 1868, construction of a sugar refinery; in 1912, a haras, or horse-breeding station. Between 1938 and 1945, it had again become part of Hungary.

You could say other things, but nothing personal. I'm using my powers carefully. I could have fallen in love with Sládkovičovo, because as with women, if you try a little, you can fall in love with any town. I just don't know what attitude Laktišová had taken toward Sládkovičovo. It could be that she had looked out the window of the bus just like this, and seen the man in front of the bistro, getting off his bike, the flap of his black pants held by a metal pincer. Under his unbuttoned jacket, you could see a striped shirt with a grandfather collar. It could be that Laktišová had seen the man, and even the truncated quotation of the empty square above the shoulders of the travelers, but she didn't say anything, and thus Sládkovičovo did not take place.

12

> The rider who stands up in the stirrups, his ass
> in the air, loses all power over the horse.

The bus took a road that passed through fields. To the side, in the wheat, three men in checkered shirts were standing. Behind them, you could see some trampled-down stalks, and I remembered, God knows why, that one day Laktišová had pointed out to me a man crouched in a field of rye: "It's so cute, look! I've seen a man peeing, but I've never seen one doing number two before!"

"Do you remember," I asked the bearded man, "that dead-drunk recruit who wanted to piss out of a window on the second floor and fell out? All night, until dawn, he was calling out down there in the grass: 'Mama!' He knew that his mother couldn't hear him, and still he was calling out: 'Mama! My dear Mama!' We could hear him, of course, but we told ourselves that it was just some dead-drunk recruit."

A grove of trees crossed the field, pulling behind it three red roofs, the rusty skeleton of a wagon, and, at the end, like a trailer, a hard, dry road through the fields. I wasn't at home here either.

13

> A fiery, nervous horse thinks endlessly of some-
> thing else. It pays attention to everything going
> on around it, except to the rider's wishes and
> orders. Every rustling, every sparrow gives it reason
> for wild behavior.

"Mama!" I said, and suddenly (it's dangerous to play with words) I remembered the day when I thought I was going to die. I was probably about ten years old.

I wasn't dying immediately. At the beginning, I had nothing more than a black point on my finger where I had pricked myself with my pen. I should specify that this wasn't the first time I had been injured. My knees were often in a pitiable state, full of purulent wounds. I had that kind of blood. But I had the worst scrapes when I was a goatherd in Štiavnica.

Goatherd . . . I'm bragging a little. I was never a goatherd. Certainly, I herded goats a number of times. During several vacations. So you could say that I used to herd goats. Well, goats? No, a kid. It had the habit of leaning its head to one side and looking around sweetly and stupidly.

Perhaps an animal is capable of self-identification . . . to the point that, fooled by its reflection in the mirror, it bites itself in the neck. But only mankind is capable of sharing a feeling, of living it in the place of another person. Of remaining oneself while becoming comprehensible in the life of another. The explanation is simple: We can only talk about other people; we're too complicated for ourselves. The kid leaned its head to one side, immobile for a moment, then made a little leap, landed on all fours, and started running. The road was called Wild Rosebush Street; like others in Štiavnica, it was cobblestone, which was good for goats, but not for me.

So I was in the middle of dying. I was looking at the tiny spot between the papillary ridges on my finger. Was it just my imagination, or was that killer spot really growing in size? It was during my biology class.

And it wasn't as if I had never hurt anybody before. In first grade, I poked a boy named Imrich Strakele in the eye. It was a funny name for a little boy. Although when it comes down to it, it would have been even funnier for a girl. Imrich Strakele was sitting in front of me. Someone said, "Imrich!" Strakele turned around . . . no, I believe it was like this (in first grade we were called by our last names): Someone cried, "Strakele!" Imrich turned and his eye knocked against my pen, which I had been pointing toward the inkwell. It was back when the desks still had penholders and inkwells. The inkwell stuck out of a hole above the bench; it was fixed there, you could say, by the brim of its hat. The blackened wood around the inkwell grew lighter each time the cleaning lady or students in detention cleaned it with emery paper, then it drank up great doses of new ink as if it were a medicinal syrup.

I don't want to say that those days were better than the present: that is neither here nor there. I mention it because we never know what is important when we're talking about another person's life. Perhaps it will be more judicious to focus on Imrich Strakele. There was something fragile about him; he said something and then smiled as if he wanted to excuse himself. . . . He had two eyes and it took so little for him to only have one. Yes, I could talk about Imrich Strakele with no problem. I could talk about the playground and its sidewalks where the pupils walked like Van Gogh's prisoners of Arles. In the corridor they gave out glasses of milk to the starving and anemic children of the postwar period. It was the "Milk for All" operation. Imrich Strakele had survived many operations; he also survived the milk distribution. It wasn't, all in all, the worst one. When he came to school, he brought a little spoon and a sugar cube on which his teacher put several drops of cod liver oil. Imrich Strakele also survived, in the same school, the Catholic operation. At the end of June, one wing of the school was still inhabited by the Ursuline order; by the first of September, when Imrich Strakele returned, there was no trace left of the nuns; on the condition, of course, that one didn't pay attention to the rumor that the toilets, filled to the brim, were an unusual farewell from the nuns. Frankly speaking, Imrich Strakele would have liked to believe those rumors; he would have been glad if the nuns had taken that kind of an attitude toward life. It's not clear whether Strakele was Catholic or Protestant. Besides, what do those words mean? If I allow myself to talk about Imrich Strakele, it's because I believe that life, if we can draw the essence from it, is one: his and mine. I'm just speculating about Imrich. That's not fair toward him. Imrich deserves his own narrator. He looks at me and smiles. "That wasn't in my eye; it was right next to it," he said, and his smile begged pardon for his slightly severe words. That dear Imrich Strakele; what a pity he doesn't exist! In fact, his name was Szakala.

But now there's that black spot. Imrich had one like it above his lip, but in relief: a beauty mark. My own isn't one of those. With love . . . no, let's not be sentimental—with interest for all that is living, I observe, with my mind's eye, the spot that extends, penetrates the epidermis, deeper and deeper, until it sketches a dark line in my scarlet blood. It's smaller on the outside now, which means there's more inside. Okay, so I pricked myself with my pen, but I've survived worse wounds. The doubtful kid looks at the stain, nods in agreement, jumps up, and starts running. I put my finger in my mouth and suck: I look at the finger; there's nothing but a little black hole. I've survived worse wounds; I forgot about my scraped knee and ran after the kid.

The kid was happy. What did it say? It said to Imrich Strakele: "Look!" Imrich turned and got poked in the eye. The wound wasn't big, but it was deep. Imrich rubbed it and ran after the kid. The kid was in favor of dialogue; it didn't believe in interior monologue; it didn't believe, in fact, that this could replace contact between the species. When it realized that Imrich wasn't running after it, it stopped. "That was something, huh?" it asked. "What's that you've got in your eye?" "Go to hell," said Imrich angrily, and he jumped, as usual, with a second's delay. This time he didn't scrape his knee, but his elbow. There were gooseberries along the fence. While standing back up, Imrich caught himself on a branch and scratched himself. Thus the gooseberries mattered to Imrich Strakele. But Imrich Strakele didn't matter to the gooseberries. That's the victory of inanimate things. The gooseberries are self-sufficient; they deserve their own narrator. What was it to them that Imrich Strakele pricked himself? They didn't worry about it. Imrich angrily picked all the berries off the bush, gobbled down the fuzzy fruit, and when he couldn't swallow any more, crushed the rest between his fingers; but even so, he didn't matter to the gooseberries. The gooseberries ceased to be, that's all. Imrich Strakele burst into tears and headed home. The kid leaned its head to one side and followed Imrich Strakele.

The kid was born on the worn, gaping, stinking floor-boards of the stable. It was completely self-sufficient. It couldn't imagine that it mattered to its mother (whose name was She-Devil), that she remembered its pain, the dark walls covered with torches, the pungent odor of urine, and the little damp body, so puny, that she licked with her tongue. The goat herself is entirely self-sufficient. Once in the middle of the night, a little body came out of her. Other things will occur later. The wardrobe that we pick at random in a furniture store will outlive us. We desire a God in order to have our own narrator, someone who follows us every moment (it's not by chance that God is an eye), faithfully, from beginning to end, someone who sees everything, understands everything, and for all that, doesn't have to forgive everything: we even don't mind if he punishes us. But when God sees us all at the same time, this whole long line of expectation, he can do nothing other than put his hands to his throat as if his collar were choking him: "Oww!"

Selfish as I am, I was imagining once how beautiful it would be to die sooner than my mother: there would be someone who knew my life like the back of her hand, someone who would be perhaps able to describe it in a sentence; just one sentence, but a definitive one.

To make a long story short, I started to die in biology class. I sucked my thumb until blood appeared; the little hole turned red. The poison was inside. I lifted my arm.

"I pricked my finger."

"Show me. Oh, that's nothing."

"I don't feel good."

"It'll pass. You were more scared than hurt."

Usually I believed everything that the schoolteacher said, so why not now? Because this time she didn't know, she didn't see the little black point that, whipping my blood with its little spermlike tail, was swimming through my bloodstream straight to my heart.

"I feel sick. I want to go home."

I didn't say that I wanted to see the doctor; they certainly would have taken me there. When Milan Ružička had appendicitis, he went straight to the hospital. They operated on him that afternoon. But that was appendicitis. He wasn't in the middle of dying. I was in the middle of dying, and I knew it. I didn't care about the doctor. I wanted to see my mother. I didn't think that she was going to help me; I wasn't such a little kid. I just wanted to die near her. If you want vodka, it should be Russian; if you want to die, it should be with Mother. As it was in the beginning, so it should be in the end. "Go home!" the teacher told me.

And what now, me or the kid? As for the kid, they cut its throat at Eastertime. The weather was rainy. The water streamed down the roof tiles, hesitating like a one-legged man coming down the staircase. The kid didn't understand about the knife, and I don't even think its death had an odor, but there's something else; a sort of death notice in the pressure of the hands that hold down the frail legs. The fingers, so playful at other moments, were seized with stiffness, and then this deep inhalation, this anguished hissing in the lungs: the kid knows. That's what's sinful in massacring goats, the unfair side of it. What should you think of the spiritual evolution of the masses, that after a thousand years has been able to invent deodorant and the electric toothbrush, but that still subjects a kid to the same distress at the moment of making its bright red blood flow through the cracks in the floorboards?

I'm just tinkering about with the kid; it deserves, it has the right to, its own narrator. How can it know? Is it perhaps simply disgusted by the hands with dirty nails, by the rancid sweat of man, does it feel squeezed by the living wall of bodies that surrounds it? Does the kid's Grim Reaper have four small hooves and a trembling goatee, does it smile with its ruminating mandibles?

Imrich Strakele, when I poked him in the eye, put his hand on the wound and said, "I know you didn't do that on purpose." He wasn't getting ready to die, and besides, he didn't die. He's still alive. The last time I saw him was at a training course for reserve officers. He didn't act very official; his face reminded me more of a girl with short hair.

The school that I had left for my encounter with death had been leveled by bombs during the war; at that time it had borne the name of Štefánik. Next to the new school, they placed the sign: NATIONAL SCHOOL FOR BOYS. In the corridors, there were red tiles on which you could slide for long distances in rubber slippers. There were also cloak-rooms, sad cages of wire mesh. I sat down in the cage and started to put on my shoes. It's strange, but I felt that I was going to miss that cage, because I had the impression—how blind and deaf self-pity can be—that it was in that cage that I had experienced the most beautiful moments of my life. What kind of experiences can you have in a cagelike cloakroom? Once they had tied my shoelaces in knots; another time, I had hit a friend on the head with the bag I carried my sneakers in. But at that moment, I remembered the long winter evenings with nostalgia: the corridors lit up with a wan light at the end of classes and the rain that dripped noiselessly on the win-dowpanes. Yes, that rain, I was going to miss it too. It's hard to die in good health, on a sunny day. Generally, ill people benefit from fatigue, but a child who's well nour-ished and full of bubbling sap can't stay in one place. How can you expect him to stay in bed! At the end, in that cage, I took leave of the school and of my friends; I felt a vague pity more for them than for myself. Once in the street, I took pity on the whole world, the autumn exhala-tions of dead leaves, the intoxicating, acrid odor from the barley fermenting in the malthouse. It wasn't until I saw, across from me, the wall of the cemetery that the feeling of regret struck my heart like a bull's-eye. The world will go on, I thought, but not me. Nobody needs me: who can I be useful to, for what? I walked down the street and cried silently, tearlessly. As usual when we're thinking about death, in my mind I went living on, though only in a spiritual form; but it was fear of the moment when they were going to cut me off from my body that really made me upset. I didn't understand that consciousness could disappear first, leaving the body to follow a step behind it.

If I had stayed until the end of class, I would have gone home with two classmates, and I wouldn't have to be dying all alone. If nothing else, there would have been our last-slap game. The one left at the end, after the others had all run away, would suffer from an absurd shame and avenge it cruelly the next day. On the way to and from school, you could always hear imprecations: "One! Two! Strike! Truce!" I felt instinctively how stupid the game was, and I hated the boys who slapped themselves three times on the fore-head, while shouting something in an absurd agreed-upon ritual. Finally, when I turned up the street behind the cemetery and they disappeared in the distance, I could go home, acting grown-up and reasonable again. Above my head, the black smoke of the brewery chimney liquefied, and in the dense body of the day a narrow crack opened by which I passed alone through the afternoon.

But today I wouldn't pass; I suddenly burst into hot tears, and I feverishly grasped my handkerchief. A gloomy little owl squealed behind the wall; or was it perhaps the cooing of a turtledove? Who knows, but for the birds and I . . .

That was how, going along the cemetery wall, I was dying with all honors. I was dying for myself. Cruelly? Absurdly? Perhaps. In any case, I was dying with all my heart, and my body didn't bother me at all; it didn't inter-vene, did not make itself felt; I was only dying mentally. Without the slightest discomfort, no sign of nausea, no pain in the injured finger. In that aspect, there wasn't a hitch.

But people can't stop existing for themselves; it would be like casting a shadow inward. It was always a little unclear to me, as if I were going to miss my own story, in the des-tiny that had fallen to me: of course, I'll continue to observe everything, I'll see others, but I won't see myself among them. I'll watch jealously through the window as the others leave for school, throwing treacherous snowballs at each other's backs, trying on brand-new ice skates in front of the Christmas tree. One sunny vacation day, there will be a nice slice of bread and butter on the kitchen table, and I won't take a bite of it; I won't have teeth, and even if I have them (certain skeletons do), I won't have an esophagus through which the food could pass into my nonexistent stomach.

That's how I was walking to see my mother, suddenly crushed by the palpable reality of the world: a crumpled-up piece of paper that the wind was blowing from one sidewalk to another, the red roof of a car that honked its horn as it crossed the intersection, healthy, and indifferent toward the world. The candy shop offered candies that would continue to stick to the palate, even if I weren't there anymore; sweet for everyone, but bitter for me. In deep despair, I stopped for the last time in front of the pillar with the cinema listings; I looked at the pictures from the movies, the beautiful women with long hair whose smile would one day become comprehensible to me, if only I would keep on living, the smile that would one day also be directed toward me, if only I would keep on living. I looked at these images that evoked a life that was full of mysteries yet certain, like the exotic name of a street which we've still never been to. That street was waiting for me somewhere, and I would not reach it; that life exists, and I am no more. I am dead. Leaning over my own corpse, I took my head in my hands; then soft as a dove, I flew on top of my white tombstone decorated with a holy image, and cried in a maudlin manner. Then, after a while, I turned away from the actress and continued on my way alongside the building of the insurance company.

There was, and still is, nothing interesting in our street: municipal baths, a dairy, a tobacco shop, a florist, a clothing shop, an entrance to a café and a theater. Nothing that could serve as an explanation, and yet, once having come to the end of this street, I already knew that I wasn't going to die. I didn't have to think about it, I knew it, and the very idea of death suddenly seemed laughable to me. When I rejoined my mother at the school where she worked, I didn't mention the injury. I just told her that they had let us out an hour early, and then I went to the library and I looked at a German book about the Sudan.

When I think now, years later, about this event, I even find a certain kind of moral lesson in it. Moral lesson is perhaps too strong a term for it, but let's say that it left a certain impression in me.

With the goats, you can appreciate this ruminating meditation that is theirs, that intelligent and quivering goatee, or even their cruel humor. Nothing of the sort with me.

With the gooseberries, you can appreciate the coherence in their pilosity, let's call it their will to displease. In me, you'd look for it in vain.

And to say a sentence about Imrich Strakele, no matter what sentence, how many wings do you have to tear off beforehand? Because he had fused with the world in one whole, softly and indistinguishably. . . . With me, there was nothing but this premature death that could make me momentarily interesting. But what to do about me, since I've started and not finished? I'm still not clear of it.

In short, I don't deserve my own narrator.

14

An experienced rider begins by searching for the cause of all his problems in himself. This is not exaggerated modesty; no, it's the perspicacity, the finesse and technique of a true rider!

" 'Mama! My dear Mama!' " I said. "How could the idea of calling his mother occur to a grown man? To take myself, for example, I don't think I would call my mother. It's easy for me to say that, because I've never fallen from the second story. But it obviously happens; even in war novels, you can read about injured men calling for their mothers. Anyway, we can expect it, we're more or less prepared for it; but the opposite! . . . That your mother would call you, that she would say: 'Come quickly, please, I've fainted and couldn't get to the telephone except by crawling on my knees.' In theory, we know that old people have all sorts of weaknesses. And even in practice, we know to face the situation: you stretch your mother out on the sofa and call an ambulance. But the problem is that if your mother calls you, you no longer have anyone to call. Certainly, you've never called her yet, so why would you do it in the future? But from now on, you have to live with the idea that, if ever . . . well, there won't be anyone to call."

"An ambulance, you see. You said it yourself."

"Of course. From a medical point of view, but that's not the question. Now I'm thinking of another kind of call. Even so, you can't start bawling: 'My dear little ambulance!' It's not a question of who will put the bandage on, but who will kiss the wound. In times past, it was the same person. But today you take your mother to a specialist; in for repair, like a radio or a vacuum cleaner. There's an example of division of labor, taken to an absurd extreme!"

When they told Mother to undress, I asked myself if I should leave. I was even hoping that the nurse would tell me outright: "Wait outside, please." But she didn't, and suddenly I didn't know if my presence could bother Mother or if it was going to reassure her instead. What's more, I thought that it could be useful to hear what the doctor said and to clarify or complete Mother's answers. So many reflections, so many hesitations, and all that, I would say today, for nothing! Because Mother may not have even realized that I was in the room, and she certainly didn't care about my presence there. In any case, with her remarkable feeling, or rather the singular instinct of the weak one for the hierarchy of power, she would have unreservedly taken the side of the doctor who, in that moment and in that space, represented the supreme authority. And rightly so, because if we give ourselves up in that way into someone's hands, it's in our interest to believe that those are the most competent hands. From that fact alone, I found myself quite precariously balanced: my mother was with her all-powerful doctor, and I was with my powerless mother. But no, I simply had nothing to do there, and, embarrassed, I turned my attention to hanging up her clothing on a wall peg. My absurd activity caught the attention of the sympathetic nurse, who told me, "You can wait outside, sir."

We're not prepared to see our mother, always so modest, undressed in front of the doctor—undressed of her clothing but also of her qualities. Of her personal modesty. Her body. Theoretically, we know it well. All in all, it's nothing but habit—it takes a little time to recognize our mother in this new disguise. Her face is always naked; we should start with the face. No, it's not very difficult, it's just that we're not prepared for it.

The body, then: it's logical, since they're going to take care of her body. This simplification is in the interest of things. No reason to object. The thing that perhaps throws us off a bit is that light odor of phenol, that polite impatience of people concentrating on the action. A functional impatience. Old people talk a lot, we all know that. Thirty years ago, she had had something like dizzy spells, in the summer; it was very hot, and the first political denunciations among schoolteachers had begun . . . we don't need to listen to that sentence to the very end, and the doctor can say: "Breathe deeply; hold your breath." The thing we're not prepared for is that you yourself don't listen to the very end. Mother cooperates without reticence. She breathes for a few moments, then she holds her breath for a few moments; without any hesitation she drops and suppresses everything that's not of interest to the doctors. She cooperates, which is certainly very wise. That's what we ourselves do at the doctor's office; we are ourselves filled with that suicidal, salutary eagerness. Why does it surprise us when we see our mother doing it? The doctors are going to help her: it's the classic story with a happy ending. . . . So what if nobody is happy at the end? It's normal, because every happy ending is based on compromise, and everyone has had to fall back on it.

15

> I have seen riders who made strange movements of the body, the chest, the shoulders, who rolled their backside, by which they wanted perhaps to demonstrate their influence and hold over the horse. We must absolutely keep ourselves from doing this. It does not look good and is contrary to the equestrian art.

Trifles. Our indignation comes basically from the fact that such a thing could occur. We're not prepared for it. Despite all cynicism, we suppose that life has a logical construction—something like a staircase or, on the contrary, some roundness that's pleasing to the eye, some sort of internal justice—that there is, as compensation for all our efforts and all the wrongs we suffered, something like a peaceful old age. Since there is such an expression, there must also have been, at least now and then, the thing that it signifies. So why the anger? Just think how easily we can accept the idea that a pigeon gives a damn about whom its droppings hit.

What matters is not death itself; we've learned to allow for death. If someone dies, above the age of sixty, we take it as something natural, like the logical consequence of having lived for sixty years. The death of Plačkova didn't surprise me in itself, only its circumstances did. I'm not afraid of saying: Since I've accepted the idea of my own death, why not accept Plačkova's death? I've never given her much thought. I knew that she was mortal, of course: her mother died, and so did her sister. It's just that . . . if my slightly outdated expression "a peaceful old age" fit anyone like a glove, it was certainly Plačkova. My mother is too close to me; she prevents me from seeing; in her case I don't dare to judge objectively.

A peaceful old age! I imagined Plačkova going shopping one sunny morning. The market is close by, just next to the cemetery. I wouldn't be able to invent a coincidence like that; I'd be ashamed to. In any case, they don't bury people in the cemetery anymore; on the contrary, they destroy the tombs. They start with those of the dead people whom nobody defends anymore, dead people who hadn't figured out in time how to obtain rich or influential descendants. Too bad for them; they just shouldn't have died so thoughtlessly.

Everyone at the market knew Plačkova. "My dear lady, try one of these gherkins. The ones here are the best quality. It's a real treat!" But Plačkova isn't attracted by pickles; she walks next to the kiosks made out of green sheet metal, and looks at the flowers. The lilies? Let's say the lilies, but there wouldn't have been many of them at the market. So maybe white carnations? She was never very hard to please, from that point of view, and now she's going to make difficulties? That's because she had gotten an idea. I like the fact that she had gotten an idea, but I would just like to know if she had herself in mind primarily, or rather other people, as she was standing in front of the flowers. But it doesn't matter. She had gotten an idea. A cat's freedom is that it doesn't get any ideas, and thus cannot betray them. A man gets an idea and his freedom—but the word isn't quite exact, perhaps—his freedom lies in the fact . . . that he sees this idea through, one is tempted to say, but that would be immodest . . . that the idea is entirely his own. And that he doesn't let anyone interfere with it.

I imagine Plačkova going shopping; or perhaps there is this horse. It's strange; I haven't thought about it for years, and suddenly it's as if I can't remember anything else from the whole war.

In a war, everyone chooses what will come back to them—even their own horrors, which are made to measure according to their possibilities. One day in the basement, next to the coal, Anna, the maid from the fifth floor, confided to me that she had seen, with her own eyes, two Russian soldiers fall off their motorcycle in front of our building. They skidded out of control, and smash! Nothing happened to the Russian boys, or hardly anything, but the motorcycle! Smashed to bits, I can't tell you! Well, yes, war is a terrible thing. I'm not making fun of Anna; I'm the same way. I remember the image of a dream, in which a plane is on fire and crashes between the apartment buildings not far away, on Lazaretska Street, and the pilot is trying in vain to escape from the burning debris. In real life, I never saw anything like that. Among my real experiences, the one that seemed the most terrible to me, because in a certain way it went against nature, was this horse in the stairwell.

I don't know what had stayed in Mother's memory. One day, she heard my father's name on the list of executed people on the radio. Luckily, it proved to be just a misunderstanding. During the bombings, in the bomb shelter, she sang folk songs to the students. Normally, she didn't used to sing very often, but she sang with all her heart, in a high voice and off-key. When we were evacuated, she used to go with her sister, under the mortar fire, to the town of Mikuláš in search of bread and news. One day, the bakery was hit by a shell that tore one of the baker's arms off, and killed his wife. The two sisters later laughed when remembering how they had jumped into the ditch not far from the bridge to escape from the shells! And how they had covered their heads with aprons to protect themselves from the fragments! Such an irrepressible, tearful laugh must have its reverse side that can't be suppressed indefinitely without paying for it. A peaceful old age, you say: after seventy years of life in the twentieth century.

16

Be friendly with your horse, but severe and
serious! The horse recognizes friendliness and
severity very well, but above all it has a particularly well developed sense for justice.

I still didn't know that the time was so near, that it would
come so suddenly, that it was already there, but theoretically,
I had admitted that my mother, losing her strength, was
going to deform and reduce her world in order to be able to
keep living in it. I had also admitted that monsters, long
kept at bay, would appear in this world from time to time. I
would have understood, for example, that shells fall in that
world, but the shells apparently weren't the worst of it.

"They threw everything outside," she breathed into my
ear when we came to see her in the hospital on Sunday.
"Pots, pans, plates, and even the little chest of drawers;
they threw it all in the garden, all lying there under the
trees. . . ." Garden? Trees? At the end, in a moment of
weakness and agony, she had revealed her real world to us.

"And their leader, this bearded Gypsy, said, 'This picture
has to go; it's not modern anymore, we'll put a Christ there
instead.' And I snapped right back, 'You can keep your
Christ; this is my house and my picture, so it's going to stay
right here.' And as if nothing had happened, he went on
with his work. 'That table is going outside, and the chest of
drawers too; that's where we're going to put a shrine to the
colt of personality.' And I told him, 'Put your colt of personality wherever you want to, but leave me alone. This is
my house.'"

That's what I wasn't prepared for. At the beginning, as
when facing someone who has a drop hanging from his
nose, I acted like I didn't notice anything. I guess I thought
that if I didn't mention it, it would pass. But it didn't.
Then I was as stubborn as a ram—with its head down:
"Nobody's tampered with anything; look at the keys, they

couldn't come into the house, everything is in its place, I went there this morning to water the flowers. . . ." To water the flowers? So they took out the pots, the chest of drawers, and I, who had never watered a flower in my life, watered the flowers. She didn't believe me, of course. She eyed me up and down with her gaze, first doubtful, then openly mistrustful, and finally she fell completely silent. What could she say, in any case, since I had to be in league with them? Fortunately—the pressure must have been too strong, or perhaps my image was already getting confused in her memory, or she had simply forgotten—she started everything all over again. At that moment, less from inspiration than fatigue, perhaps also dragged along despite myself by the suggestive world of that story, I said: "I'd really like to see anyone making a mess in your apartment. Just let them try. Don't worry; I'll take care of those hooligans in five seconds flat." It was more or less in that spirit, and when I saw (I swear I didn't look for it on purpose) a hopeful but still hesitant light in her eyes, I let myself be carried away by a kind of euphoric logorrhea: "I'll kick the shit out of them; that's what I'm going to do. We've dealt with tougher guys. They'll clear out fast enough, the bastards." From the very fact that she hadn't reprimanded me for that indecent word, I could tell how much she was concentrating on the essence, on that muscular and carefree tone, and leaving words aside, she was reaching directly for the image. "Kick the shit out of them?" she repeated, half questioning, half asking, and pronounced it with an infantile joy to celebrate this moment when the two of us were able to say vulgar words so boldly. "I'll kick the shit out of them and throw them down the stairs," I confirmed. "I'll whip them. You don't have anything to be afraid of."

I settled it in less than two minutes; I didn't even need to roll up my sleeves. And with a smile that was meant to excuse me before myself and before the assembled company—if only the guy on the next bed had heard it—but which meant for her that I was lightly getting rid of that minor matter. She smiled too, uncertainly at first, as if wondering whether her muscles were still up to the task, and put her hand on top of mine. Such a wise palm, such an intelligent hand! She must have known all that time, and with that silent applause she wanted to reward me all the same, to reassure me in my senseless and hilarious despair. Mother's hands, sensible and attentive until the bitter end; the taciturn and permanent commentary of her thin fingers. . . . She never mentioned the intruders again.

17

> Nowadays one demands that the horse under
> its rider pass over every obstacle, while going this
> way and that.

But there was worse. You can imagine a broken arm, and with a little effort, you can also understand gallstones or appendicitis, but how can you picture a sprain or a fracture of that which is essential, of that which we address ourselves to, of that which is unique . . . being? We're not prepared for it. That face which had to begin by discovering us in some remote past or perhaps returned to us from some distant future, in any case at the cost of a great effort—that face, jars of jam between the windowpanes, and beyond the window, a cemetery. (I wouldn't have been able to invent something like that; I would have been ashamed. Well, yes, there's a cemetery next to the hospital, but they don't bury anyone there anymore.) It was after the operation. Sometimes Mother even slipped on her slippers and went to style her hair in the bathroom; on the way there, she informed me that the girl sleeping on the bed in the corner would like to study at the university. Such a nice girl; wouldn't it be possible to do something for her? Moments of brightness. But more often there were complaints from nurses,

"Granny doesn't want to eat anything," to which Mother would react with a contrite, absentminded smile, as if she couldn't recognize herself in the picture they painted. She moved her lips silently and I had to lean over, a little closer, right next to her mouth: "Take me home!"

The art of diverting the conversation. "Are you doing all right?" What a stupid question, and the worst part is that it was sincere, I mean that you would sincerely wait for her to answer yes. I would even take it as the symptom of an improvement—not the fact that she was feeling well, that could have been a lie, but that she would remember this game, that she would accept it again. She starts to smile again and you celebrate, up to the moment when you become aware of the treachery of that smile, of its double game. "I'll tell you later," she mumbles with her voiceless lips, "at home. But take me there quickly!"

"Tomorrow, maybe. While you're waiting for that, you have to eat well, to get your strength back." Lying isn't difficult; it comes out all by itself, like a cry of pain, and in fact it's not a matter of lies: she remembers "tomorrow," you remember "maybe." Lying isn't a problem; the problem is that she believes you, while she has to know that her departure depends neither on her nor on you, but on the doctors. And perhaps she doesn't believe you—didn't the doctors say she was trying to escape in her bathrobe and slippers? That means you've lost her trust. But yet, on the next visit she gives you a big smile and tries again: "Couldn't we go home today?" She's ready to team up with anyone against everyone; Machiavellian in her terrible solitude, in her powerlessness, she nods when you explain to her slowly and patiently that she has to get well in the hospital before everything else. She acts like she believes this stupid story. You feel relieved, you believe that you've already persuaded her, then she lifts herself up on her elbows, brings her yellowish face close to you tenderly, and cries into your ear with her little voice: "But why? What have I done?" And still, that isn't the worst;

with a little goodwill, you could consider it a reproach addressed to God or destiny. But she immediately makes herself clear: "I told them, shoot me now. Why don't you shoot me right away? Why are you torturing me? That doesn't do any good; if I knew anything, I would have told you a long time ago."

Maybe they would have had to explain to her the reason for her operation with more patience; maybe they would have had to warn her more energetically; it was also possible that they had warned her, but for nothing; in her world there was no operation, there were only cross-examinations. Above, there was a large empty room, the execution chamber. All night she heard gunshots right above her head. That's the world in which she lived, all alone, because you weren't much help to her either. On the contrary, it was you who had taken her there, without the least sign of resistance, and you who had insisted, under futile pretexts, that she stay there. She didn't make the slightest complaint to you, she stifled them all within herself, because she wanted to hold on to the hope that one day, perhaps really. . . . You teamed up with them, it was clear, but just because of that, one day, perhaps really. . . . She stayed in bed, apparently immobile, but constantly on the alert, vigilant, because in a world like that where you didn't survive except thanks to absolute cunning, you had to be as shrewd as a monkey.

I was there when a friend came to see her. She was an old friend, the closest of the friends she had left; they had known each other for forty years, or even fifty? For longer than I can remember. Mother listened to her with an indifferent smile on her lips, and didn't say anything.

We had warned the friend, of course. She was prepared for a lot of things but apparently not for everything.

"Do you recognize me?" she asked at the end, upset. "Do you know who I am?"

Mother gave her a quick look. Her cunning smile grew a long mustache, curved like the handlebars of a bicycle.

"I recognize you."

"And what's my name?" the friend asked, because she was a real, courageous friend. She was ten years older than Mother and had lived through a lot of things. She had survived two world wars, the premature death of her husband . . . but what good would it do to enter into such detail? She had lived through more than eighty years in the twentieth century. She would survive this meeting with Mother too.

"Tell me yourself," Mother answered, still smiling. If there is a truly childish treachery, we were having a demonstration of it then. The friend gave up: "Marta."

"Marta." Mother closed her eyes for a moment, as if she were listening to what was going to move inside her. Or maybe she was learning the name by heart. "What do you think, that I don't know you're Marta?" she concluded triumphantly.

That's how it was in the world she lived in, in a world where she could only retreat more and more deeply. A short time afterward, we were nothing more than vaguely familiar tones. She couldn't make out the melody anymore.

18

> What is absolutely important are the legs and
> the back. The rest is nothing but an agreeable
> or disagreeable complement.

For those who would be interested: The bearded man and his companion got off at Nitra. The bus stopped there for fifteen minutes and we had the time to get a coffee at the snack bar. While I was alone at the register with the bearded man, I asked him (with a good-natured smile, I thought): "Your girlfriend?" For a moment, it seemed as if he didn't know what it was all about, and he even glanced around questioningly, then said: "A colleague." Make of it what you will. Personally, I had the impression that with that response, he was pushing me softly away, as if he were already building a fence around himself, over which he was going to shake my hand for the last time; or perhaps he had felt that I was going to use him, and then let him drop without a second thought?

The bearded man (after all, we know his attitude to literature) didn't read Shakespeare, because he thought that the Bard had nothing to say about him, but there's a sentence in Shakespeare: "The Moor has served; the Moor may leave."

A colleague . . . you see, he hadn't even introduced me to her, we had only vaguely waved to each other as a form of greeting, as if we were both shooing away the same fly . . . for that colleague, I had a very simple explanation. She was an angel.

Personally, I believe in the existence of angels; since cultural attachés can exist, why not angels? I'd just like to know whether the bearded man knew about it, and if so, how he had been able to . . . or maybe she wasn't an angel for him, although she was for me? Did the angel have an extra job as the bearded man's girlfriend, the way some workers are also stewards in the trade union? Or perhaps it was just the opposite, and it was the girlfriend who had taken the initiative to be an angel in her off-hours? Nothing would have surprised me, at least not in this story. But all the same, I was astonished.

If I had the power to do this, which I don't, I'd offer the bearded man his own narrator. As for the colleague . . . angels don't need one. They have their own narrator up in heaven.

19

> All these stories about the suggestive effect of the human look on the horse are nothing but fairy tales. No man has ever been able to stop a galloping horse simply with a look.

The bus is, of course, a way out. Who could have come up with such a stupid sentence? But all in all, why not, in any

case at the beginning: that initial jolt, that change of position. . . . It was like when I left the hospital; from the staircase to the tarmac courtyard, then once past the wide-open
gate, each time I felt an intense relief. Afterward, I was
ashamed of it, because we aren't ready for that. The idea of
feeling relief when I left my mother was unbearable to me,
to the point that I had to look for another explanation, even
an untrue one: Leaving the hospital, I felt relieved because I
was no longer directly confronted with my own powerlessness. White canvas overshoes that made me walk clumsily . . .
but no, it wasn't about that. I slipped a hundred crowns to
the nurse. An absurd, instinctive movement. . . . Besides, in
a moment of clarity, Mother had whispered to me: "Did you
give the nurse something? The one with brown hair, she's so
nice." I gave something to the brown-haired one, and also to
the blond one, but not because I thought that my mother
was going to have anything extra, for that ever-smiling nurse
would have smiled at my mother even without the hundred
crowns. It would have taken absolute willpower, an almost
inhuman intransigence, for the nurse to sulk at my mother
just because she hadn't gotten her hundred crowns. As if
every patient, or in fact everyone, didn't spontaneously provoke their own echo in other people. I fed my mother some
apricots in syrup, because it seemed to me that she liked
them a lot. I fed them to her, thinking stupidly that she
hadn't touched the plate of dumplings in sauce that was on
the nightstand ("Granny doesn't want to eat anything!")
simply because she didn't like the hospital food. Mother
clenched her teeth shut, and the syrup dribbled down her
chin, falling on the pink collar of her nightgown; one drop
even fell out of the spoon. . . . I surprised myself by thinking—or was it, perhaps, a reflex, a signal that I managed to
halt as it came out of my mind?—"If you don't stop pushing
this spoon away right now, you'll get a smack."

I wasn't ashamed of giving a bribe; I'm old enough not
to be afraid of words anymore. Back when I was around

eight years old, it wasn't like that: I remember with what priggishness, which was actually just the reverse side of my desire for an absolute trust, I weighed every one of Mother's words, to see if it corresponded to reality: every figure of speech, every hyperbole. It was enough for her to say "We waited a half hour for the tram" for me to correct her: "It was only ten minutes." And then, when she wasn't very tired, she knew how to reprimand me sharply: "Are you trying to say that I'm lying?" Like every ordinary family, we usually used the word "fibbing." But no, for that single solemn occasion, she reserved that terrible, magical, imprecatory word "lie," which left me in awe.

Nowadays no one can scare me with the word "bribe"; the problem is that in reality, if I don't try to get any advantage . . . it's difficult to dodge such questions. The nurse does what she can, what she wants to, according to her character and her mood: the conscientious one is conscientious, the disorganized one is disorganized. And then, Mother doesn't particularly want the nurse's smile. Mother wants to go back home. So what does all this gesticulating mean? Do I want to win the favors of the god of illness with this offering? Do I want to prove to somebody—myself, for example—that I don't skimp when it comes to my mother? Do I want to repay the nurse for doing what I should have been doing? Or perhaps I simply wanted to say with a clear conscience: "I've done everything I could have done." Have I, really?

The next day we took Mother home.

20

> Feeding time must be scrupulously respected,
> because regular feeding contributes greatly to
> the training of the young horse and to keeping
> the old horse in good shape.

We took Mother home from the hospital so quickly because we were hoping she was going to revive here and now in the milieu that was familiar to her. Yes, yes, the pots, the pans, the plates, everything was in order, even the little chest of drawers in the bedroom, and yet. . . .

Nighttime was the worst. Of course, at night everything is worse; every shadow is darker. I went to bed in the bedroom, on the floor next to the door. I took a lamp with me and left it on, so that Mother and I could orient ourselves quickly in the dark—it was all the same to my mother, because she didn't know where she was in any case—and I kept alert for noises from her duvet. There you have it. At first, under the table—it was the horizon that my position offered me—I saw a leg groping around for a slipper, then a hand coming to the rescue. Very slowly, with apprehension, as if for the first time in its life. Then the other leg. So we were going to go for a walk. I kicked away my duvet. Mother was sitting on her bed—I heard a sigh. Had she remembered something, or was it simply her body that had sighed? Suddenly, before I could get up, the hand reappeared under the table and brutally pulled the slipper off the foot. Good heavens! She was sometimes able to spend an hour just putting on and taking off her slippers. In any case, I had that impression, because at night every second is a second longer.

But there were also our walks, of course. I walked a step behind her, and tried to guess which way she would be going. She didn't respond to questions, and if she responded, we didn't understand anything. I always ended up taking her to the toilet; that was the limit of my imagination. I did it in the hope, how can I explain it, the hope of having understood her, at least in that way. I waited for her to smile at me; that would have been a good beginning. But who can go to the toilet twenty times in one night, with a smile? Sometimes, I let her do it herself, because I didn't want to get up, or I simply didn't wake up in time. I found her standing, confused, in the kitchen or the bathroom. I say "confused," but that's my point of view, because

Mother, in her own world, had perhaps come to the very place where she wanted to be.

During the day, the thing I dreaded the most was feeding. Maybe the word "feeding" isn't very nice, but in this case it's precise. Mother showed, on the one hand, a fairly strong resistance to eating in general, and on the other hand, a specific resistance to the dish we would offer her. The two were automatic, and it was necessary to overcome them, but Mother had a rich repertory of means of passive resistance at her disposal, ranging from disgusted grimaces to holding the food in her mouth, or just turning her head away constantly. At the end of several attempts, we were able to connect approximately, in an attitude of joyful determination, a sort of energetic patience that presented the greatest chance of success in feeding. I considered three spoonfuls of meat and egg broth a success, and sometimes it was so hard to catch the transparent phlegm of egg white in a spoon!

This energetic patience, or rather this joyful determination, was like a big ganglion in my chest, a lumpish nodosity, made up of who knows what internal secretions, that I had to assemble in myself and thicken with the effort of my will. For this reason, each time the feeding took me at least a half hour of preliminary concentration. I guess we had both feared this moment, the only difference being that I couldn't show it.

How Mother's grimaces made me laugh, and how my laugh incited her to invent new ones! In fact, she expected it! Mother knew her own talent, but even so, she was happy when I confirmed it. And yet she had never trained in front of a mirror! Each time, she must have had an ideal grimace in mind that she was trying to imitate. I was happy when she laughed at herself, because an attitude like that showed a certain aloofness, and what's more, when she laughed, she swallowed the piece of food that she had been holding in her mouth. But in any case, laughing or not laughing, it usually wasn't more than three spoonfuls. After the feeding, both of us were tired.

Okay, I could imagine myself with a large ganglion in my chest (which is nothing but a metaphor, of course, an impatient ellipsis), but compared to Mother, who was never, from head to toe, anything other than a single node of will, strong enough to resist the chop of an axe, I was nothing but a dilettante in the matter. In my moments of lucidity, I rather thought that in her world, where I was nothing but a hazy silhouette, without contours, she had given me a role that allowed her to act like a child. It's the only honorable solution for a weak person, because weakness is a natural thing in a child. Crazy tall tales. But really, why not? A changing silhouette, without contours. In her world, she was the only real and living person. For her, we were only raw material that she used to create other characters in her world. I think that in me, she brought together several people with similar traits, people whom she felt the same way toward, and the predominant place was occupied by her father. I don't mean by this that she really took me for her father (I never knew my grandfather; he died when my mother was a young girl), but then again she never showed, I must say, that she recognized me as her son: she never called me by my name. It was perhaps due to that basic and profound uncertainty she showed when her friend came to visit. But finally, what would she have been able to call me, since in the place of words her mouth only let out some sounds: *yabblah-kabblah-babblah, keery-beery-beem?* Then she burst out laughing and finished, saddened, by shaking her head sorrowfully!

21

If the horse is afraid of something, instruct it
that in this case, its fear is groundless. Encourage
it in a forceful but pleasant fashion to come

A HORSE UPSTAIRS, A BLIND MAN IN VRÁBLE

closer. If you ever whip it, you will only increase
its fear, because it will be convinced that the
blow comes from the object that it dreads.

"You'll certainly go to heaven," I told Mother one day,
when she had just darned a large hole in my sock. That
sock should have been thrown in the garbage, not mended.
I was so moved by this absurd, useless task that I said without thinking: "You'll certainly go to heaven."

"Let's hope you're telling the truth," she said. "There will
certainly be a welcoming or review committee, and you
know what that means. I've never been able to put things
straight with the authorities. In the time of the Slovak State,
they held me up to public disgrace because I didn't go to
Mass every Sunday; in the fifties, it was hell because they
reproached me for not having repudiated religion. Who
knows what they're going to come up with next."

During the worst period, I pulled some strings and got
a psychiatrist to come and take stock of her condition.
Mother heard a strange voice out in the hallway and sensed
the importance of the moment. She dashed into her bedroom, threw off her bathrobe and nightgown, and stood in
front of the wardrobe, naked and trembling. I believed
that she couldn't choose quickly which dress to wear on
that solemn occasion, or that she had already forgotten what
she had come in there for, so I gave her the first dress that
came to hand, and I brought her back out into the living
room. The psychiatrist sat Mother down in the armchair
and asked her to tell him the "Our Father" in German. I
don't know why he assumed that Mother knew the "Our
Father" in German, but she cleared her throat several times
and very, very slowly, said: "*Vater unser . . .*" and that was
all. I didn't hear the other questions, because I left them
alone. Later in the entryway the psychiatrist explained that
the prognosis was poor, that Mother's state was hopeless,
and that we would have to find a nursing home for her. As

soon as the door closed behind him, Mother, so moved that she could speak again, asked me: "How did that man get to know our father?" It doesn't matter; it was the first reaction, still confused; a moment later, when she was putting on her nightgown, with her mouth half hidden in her collar, she said: "You see, I told you; they wouldn't want me in heaven." I couldn't see if she was smiling as she said that.

"I propose assumption instead of old age." What did I really expect? I imagined that Mother would go out on the balcony and suddenly, in the middle of a deep silence, peacefully start to rise up. It would be without farewells, without useless ceremonies, and even if I would want to say something, she wouldn't hear me anymore. And what would I be able to tell her, anyway? "Take your coat, so you're not cold on the way"? I wasn't reckoning with death; I was simply thinking that certain administrative procedures were going to be eliminated.

22

The horse must have heart, that is,
be courageous.

As I said, this is a story with a happy ending, and so what if none of the characters are happy? The main thing is that the ending is happy. It was a summer morning, I was sitting on the bus, my mother had gone to the market where the day before yesterday, but not today, she could have met Plačkova. She certainly would have recognized her, although her arms were overflowing with flowers.

Plačkova, each time we saw her, was as suffused with joy as others are suffused with redness. She couldn't help herself. "Oh, my shaggy little darling," she had the habit of saying to my mother. Or perhaps: "Where are you running to like that, my sweaty little dear?" Seeing you come out of a cesspool, she certainly would have called out, "How are you, my little poopykins?" She saw everything, and didn't try to pretend she hadn't, but in spite of that, we could be sure she still felt warmly toward us.

Plačkova was an old maid, but it didn't show. The old maid was her elder sister, and Plačkova was in fact the young old maid. She wasn't one of those people who had flunked out of the school of sainthood and were bitter about their failure for the rest of their lives. She was like the angels—they don't have any prejudice against sex; they're just asexual. Let's just say that in the place of sex, they have wings. It's strange that I know her so little; she was, for me in any case, a woman with no personal problems; each time I saw her, she talked to me about myself, not about herself. The only time she showed us her anguish was that time with the horse.

When the Red Army liberated Bratislava, the soldiers were lodged in our apartment building. We also had a lieutenant lodging with us; his name was Magda, a funny name for a lieutenant. I remember it because he left us a photograph with his autograph: under the cloth cap, the soft face of a girl with short hair. Most of the soldiers were living on the fourth floor. Why the fourth floor, I don't know; perhaps it had the most space, or perhaps they liked having a nice view. One day, one of these soldiers decided to go up to his apartment with his horse. At the time everyone thought, of course, that he was drunk, but these days when I look at the cars parked on the sidewalk, I tell myself that perhaps he was perfectly clearheaded. At that time, nobody stole cars yet, because there weren't very many of them. There were more horses.

There were so many horses that even for the city children, a horse in itself was nothing unusual. We all knew the Silesian bay with the white star that pulled the blue postal wagon. But a horse in our tiled hallway, on our concrete staircase! We all rushed there right away and hung back at a respectful distance, because a horse on the staircase, that's impressive; it's enormous, and it makes the staircase seem tiny.

The horse—but it's *a posteriori* that I'm trying to decipher my amazement—such as we knew it on the street, the civil-servant horse, was characterized by its balance, its regularity, and its almost mechanical movement; only from time to time, you would have said that he was encouraging himself with a stronger motion of his head, but it could be that he was only doing that to keep time with his step or even that he was driving away a haunting memory. The horse on our staircase was a completely different kind of beast, a wild species, it seemed to us, furious to the point of madness, to the point of losing all coordination, seemingly contradicting itself in its movements. It moved its front legs frenetically, to the point of having huge knots on the top of its shoulders, while its back legs were braking, pressing against the edge of the steps. Then, suddenly, it relaxed and made a desperate jump; its horseshoes pedaled in empty space and crunched on the concrete like a knife on a plate. At first we shrank back, terrified by those larger-than-life noises. The soldier's curses and encouragements resounded above, where we couldn't see; once or twice, he also appeared below, hitting the horse on its behind or trying to push it; we could only see his black boots, and then he disappeared. It's astonishing how that staircase, which we had gone up and down several times every day, suddenly seemed foreign to us, as if we couldn't recognize it anymore. But we had lived in that apartment building through the bombardment of the nearby Apolka refinery, and it hadn't changed, only the sky had been strangely colored for a moment; we had lived there through other air raids, and it was still the same building, only the cellar, usually uninhabited, with its silent pile of coal behind the partitions that let the light through, had been filled with low conversations, as if the people were merely waiting for someone to come and bring a meeting of building residents to order.

On the first floor—the soldier had to stop there; he hadn't been able to turn with the horse, but he found a solution. He rang at one apartment and pushed the horse halfway through the open door, then rang at the opposite apartment and pushed the rear end of the horse through that door, after which they could move onward—at least to the first floor, where the horse stopped for a moment, we saw the hairs quiver on its flank, and then a jerky and incoherent movement, like an uncontrollable nervous tic, and we still couldn't understand a thing, we thought that it was possessed by the devil. On the second floor, the soldier started the doorbell procedure all over again, and then on the third floor . . . Plačkova wasn't aware of the technical difficulties with the horse; she only understood that a dead-drunk soldier was trying to enter her apartment; she blackened her face with soot, went out on the balcony, and screamed: "Help, save me! They want to rape me!" In the end, the concierge went up, swearing like a tinker, and threw the soldier and his horse out into the street.

Plačkova attended Mass, but didn't make a big deal about it. I never heard her mention God except in expressions like "Thank God!" and "God help us!" If she went to church (I know she did, because I saw her there when I was a kid), she also went to confession—with her sins, I would have had no problem going to confession myself.

As for the horse, at close range it seemed to be angry, and it's taken thirty-nine years to realize that it was actually afraid—because it seemed incredible that a horse could be afraid of a staircase, which even a child isn't afraid of. We all knew right away that Plačkova was afraid; she was afraid of being raped, but she was even more afraid of dying; if not, she would have jumped from her balcony, you see! And if she went to confession, she must have known that suicide is a mortal sin.

Thirty-nine years later, Plačkova went to have a chat with the neighbor, and on that occasion, left her bankbook there for safekeeping. As she said, she was going to leave for several days; she didn't want anyone to steal it from her apartment, because it was the money she had set aside for her burial. Thirty-nine years later, Plačkova bought some flowers at the market, put them in the bathroom, filled the bathtub with water, lay down in it, and slit her wrists.

Without having thought about it too much, I knew that when it came down to it, Plačkova was mortal. But to slit her wrists like that; it was so unfeminine! It's so cruel, disdainful, like spitting into someone's face. And one has the right to expect a little more modesty from an old maid, even a young old maid. By the way, had she stepped into the bathtub with her bathrobe on? My bloodless little dear!

No, we're not prepared for that, that peaceful, silent, closed hatred: because there's something hateful in those cut veins, a sort of categorical, even tyrannical, refusal. It's not that I assume I could have changed anything at all about her decision, or influenced her feeling about life—by visiting her more often, for example. Besides, I had never visited her at all; at the most, we had exchanged a few words in our chance meetings in the entrance to the apartment building, or in the elevator. And even if I had visited her a few times, what would I have told her? I'm not ashamed of lying, but I can't invent an exhilarating lie. Even when Mother turns her head hopefully to the draft of air as soon as I open the door, and asks, "What's new?" the only thing I can tell her is, "Nothing." Should I tell her: "Tomorrow I mean to fall in love with the town of Vráble"? So it's she who overwhelms me with her news: that the doctor's office is still crowded, that her butcher has given her a bad cut of meat again, and that it's terrible how many people there are in the streets on weekday mornings. That they still don't know whether they're going to leave Dad's gravestone, or whether they're going to remove the cemetery altogether, that she can't stand this uncertainty anymore, that she went to make some inquiries at the crematorium just to find out if they would really incinerate Dad's mortal remains in case she had him exhumed, and in a very friendly and warm manner they answered yes, naturally, but an exhumation is a very onerous thing and this would lead to some annoyances, it was so long since your husband passed away, wasn't it, almost forty years ago, so leave his grave in peace, and bring an urn, if you like, we'll find you some ashes. At first, you don't know what to think of such news: Was she still delirious? But why only on this very point? Besides, it was enough to look out the window: most tombstones are just flung on the ground, and on my father's grave you can also see the marks of indelible paint. At the end, I couldn't think of anything anymore: "Well, it's still a beautiful sunny day today." She followed my look, blinked, and said, "The windows are dirty again."

No, as for Plačkova, I have a clear conscience, yet her act concerns me—I was a constituent part, if only a completely marginal one, of her world, and thus she rejected me at the same time as that world. As if she had wanted to tell me: "I don't want to be in your world anymore." It would be useless to strike back: My world? Why is it mine? Well, yes, it is—how I love this cheap dialectic, but there's nothing to be done—if only by the fact that I left so few imprints on it. The old lady shamed all of us with her vehemence and her ferocity. I imagine that old age is something round, obliging, something that evaporates, little by little, with time. But I wasn't prepared for this.

Perhaps because of that very brutality—but there's no need to explain; it's entirely logical that I wasn't going to mention Plačkova in front of Mother. I ask myself whether our solicitude is always so imprecise, so groping. "Have you heard what happened to Plačkova?" she asked me as soon as I opened the door. "She slit her wrists." I told her I knew about it, but she didn't let herself get flustered; she kept on talking calmly and slowly, because she had to take out the ironing board, cut the onions, light the gas, melt the lard, and so on. "Look at this lousy piece of meat, and I walked all over for it. It seems that she had flowers all around her." This serenity intrigued me: Was it the ego-centrism of an old person, or just the satisfaction of having survived, where others could not? Or did she have the impression that Plačkova had spoken for her, with her act, and that she had freed her from that duty? Or that Plačkova, since she had left earlier, was going to keep a place for her in the next world? In any case, I couldn't really explain Mother's serenity to myself.

As for me, there was that horse on the staircase, the sunny summer morning, the flowers . . . especially the flowers. Suddenly I remembered that when I was a child, I had seen drowned kittens floating in the stream. I already knew that kittens were drowned sometimes, that wasn't what mattered; two or three years later—"you wanted a cat, so you take care of them now"—they will send me to the Váh River with a cardboard box. That wasn't what mattered; but those kittens—there were two of them, still blind—were wearing ribbons around their necks. One pink, the other blue. I couldn't say right away what was bothering me; a single idea, imprecise and vague, had crossed my mind: What a waste! To put ribbons on kittens that you're going to drown! Nowadays, such perversity would even make me throw up, and yet it's so human: to embellish, to decorate yourself for a special occasion, even if the occasion is death! Well, yes, how can we imagine death if we don't put a ribbon on it?

The kittens hadn't put the ribbons on themselves, of course. They didn't go to the stream, breathe deeply, close their blind eyes, and jump. Plačkova had gotten an idea. Lilies or white carnations? I don't know; I wasn't there. I didn't go to see her because I didn't have anything to say to her; I just saw the police sealing the door: they seal doors with an adhesive paper tape. She had gotten an idea; perhaps she thought she would be floating on the crystalline waters of her bathtub surrounded by flowers; but her idea disappeared with her.

In the past, Plačkova had been afraid of death. She had also been afraid of rape, but that's understandable; indeed, when you have wings instead of a sex, you can't imagine rape, and it is the unimaginable that is the strongest source of horror. I don't mean to make fun of her, but I don't want to feel sorry for her either—in any case, the horse had been even more frightened.

What a merry, pleasant story, full of the best intentions, yet with so many horrors on every side! The soldier—the soldier was doing his duty, of course, obeying orders, but at the same time, because such is human nature, at the same time, to make this plane of necessity more bearable, to be able to identify with it, if only partially, he raised the vault of his own thought upon it—the soldier formed the idea that he was chasing away, suppressing evil, bringing to people, and thus to Plačkova too, something joyful that you have to welcome with open arms, with flowers, a sort of . . . I don't know how he would have named it for himself. The soldier loves his horse, he doesn't want to lose it, he imagines that it will be better off on the fourth floor, that it will be safer there.

Plačkova believed in God; she was a pious person, as they say. Thirty-nine years later . . . the problem isn't that she died, but that she had to take care of it all herself. When a person has found God in this impious world, has cultivated him and kept in shape—well, she would have rightfully deserved that the Good Lord take her up to heaven. But in this case, he evidently screwed up.

I appreciate that Plačkova had gotten an idea and that, despite her piety, she knew how to see it through. She didn't believe in the priest's anger: indeed, someone who takes the part of acting directly doesn't need an interpreter: if necessary, God himself will give her a good dressing-down. Or perhaps she'll give God one, who knows?

I had imagined in the past that life had a logical construction, that it was a regular curve, a very aesthetic one. "I propose assumption in place of aging," I said yesterday to the State Pension Office; what was I expecting? If even God, collapsing under the weight of requests, only expedites group demands, wars and genocides, what could I expect from the administration? Well, yes, I had even thought, on the bus, that I would have to send a complaint on that subject, as if I didn't know how they were going to respond. They're going to give the excuse that the white-haired old pensioner gave me incorrect information. All things considered, I wasn't reckoning with death; I was simply thinking that certain administrative procedures were going to be eliminated.

In the time when Mother was still living in her own world, she stole an empty pack of cigarettes when nobody was looking and wrote on it in trembling capital letters: HELP! I'M LOCKED UP IN HERE! Then she threw the packet through the half-open window into the courtyard. I could see that she was throwing something, so I went down to see what it was. Those two sentences upset me, because Mother used to have beautiful, energetic handwriting. But on the other hand, it was encouraging that she had decided to communicate with the outside world, with the other world; that she hadn't abandoned hope. These days she wasn't interested in cigarette packets anymore. Sometimes I tell myself, as long as her consciousness is still alert and eager I would put up with any mutilation of her body. As long as her consciousness can still walk without crutches—or even with crutches, as long as it still wants to go for walks! As for the body, I would even carry it in my arms.

23

An experienced rider can look at the countryside from atop his horse; nevertheless, he must pay attention to the path and always be ready to help his mount.

A HORSE UPSTAIRS, A BLIND MAN IN VRÁBLE

The bus is evidently a way out, but a grown man must have a pretext for every act; let's say that I left to fall in love with the town of Vráble.

The Tesla radio tower rose from the plain like a rough shout, and the bus entered Vráble without announcing the station. At the bus station, they only gave three or four minutes, so it had to be love at first and last sight. Let's say I wanted to see Vráble as Laktišová had seen it, through her eyes; I wanted us to have something in common; if nothing else, then at least Vráble. I wanted . . . I thought that you could reach Laktišová by passing through Vráble. Frankly, I don't know what I was expecting.

To make a long story short, I looked. There was a single-story yellow building with two girls under the awning, as if they wanted to take shelter from a rain that hadn't yet materialized. Two young women. One of them glanced quickly at the bus, without curiosity: weary eyes that had seen everything. Given her age, you'd find it hard to believe that her eyes had seen so much, I'll say, and what's much worse is that they've seen everything, that's to say, to stick to that which concerns us, all the buses that stop here right on schedule, all the chance misadventures behind their windows, and above all, the worst of all, all the forms of "self" taking shelter under the awning from a nonexistent rain. Once we're confronted with such a look, it's no use giving epochs the most sublime, winged names. The look was telling me: You, arbitrarily and countlessly repeatable you, and although I realized it was only my imagination, although I knew that the girl was looking beyond me, and in the best case she saw only her own reflection (but isn't it the same thing?) in the window of the bus, at one moment I found that look so unbearable. . . . I wanted so much to disrupt it in its omniscience, to disturb it in its despair— that is, in my despair. . . . In short, I stuck out my tongue at her. I was sitting next to the window, I turned my head and

. . . but what good are all these sentences? She didn't see me. In any case, she didn't show it. At which the bus moved away, the door slammed shut, and I turned away, with my tongue still stuck out like an idiot. . . . She'll have to grow old without my help. Yes, that was my first thought, impertinent and vain, and I did not realize that it was true the other way around too.

Before turning onto the main road, the bus stopped for a moment to give the right of way. There was also another obstacle. On the main road, they had torn out the cobblestones and were putting down a tarmac surface. (For those who might be interested: The road was named after the Red Army, and the pavement dated from 1934. I know that because the date was marked on the lighter cobblestones.) The time offered was extra, and I didn't want to waste it. I looked avidly through the window, and saw what you can see through a bus window.

At the corner of the street, right next to the sidewalk, there was a blind man. He was wearing a light summer suit and a Panama hat with a black ribbon. The open collar of his white shirt spread over the back of his jacket. He had a gray mustache, slightly yellowed above his upper lip. He was leaning with his cane on the edge of the sidewalk. His lips were moving, but in the bus, with the engine running, you couldn't tell if he was actually saying something.

There was nobody around, only on one side the low decorative walls in front of the little villas, and on the other side a vague dusty landscape with piles of broken bricks, rolls of cable, and rusty scrap iron. In the distance, as if it were emerging from the fields, the Tesla tower was pointing toward the sky. There were cars going down the road, the bus was waiting, and at the edge of the sidewalk, an old man in a light summer suit moved his lips without stopping, regularly, as if he were reciting litanies or swearing. But it could be that he was in the middle of telling his life story. We waited at that intersection and I repeated everything to myself, just to be sure:

There were heavy branches hanging down from the gardens, and at the corner of the street, under those branches, a blind man in a light summer suit. He was moving his lips and watching over the edge of the sidewalk with his white cane. His apparent immobility seemed full of patience, yet his lips betrayed an overflow of hatred. At the corner of the street, in Vráble, a blind man, and next to him, in Vráble, at the corner of the street, a bus; the latter pulls away and immediately thereafter, although you can't see it anymore, the blind man leaves too. They're next to each other in two different chronologies: in five minutes, the bus will be in Telince and the blind man will be in Vráble. At a quarter to eleven, the bus will be in Dudince and the blind man will be in Vráble. At seven in the evening, the bus will be in Bratislava, the blind man in Vráble. The blind man will die in Vráble, while the bus . . . so much for Vráble. Love won't happen on the bus, only a brief sharp pain, a vertigo of nothingness.

But there was something in that scene that I call *ikebana,* something absurd and beautiful. I've often thought about it since then, but I haven't found any explanation. Would I have envied the blind man? Okay, I envied him, but for what, really? Because after all, it's not set in stone that I won't develop a cataract someday . . . but after all, I could poke my eyes out anytime. So what did I envy him for? For that blind, sleepwalking confidence, with which he lasts in its delimited space? For the furious, self-sufficient frustration of inaudible lips?

Before turning on to the main road, the bus stopped to give the right of way. I ran up to the door and asked the driver:

"Could you open it for me? I'd like to get off."

At a quarter to eleven, the bus was in Dudince and the blind man was in Vráble. I was in Bratislava.

24

It would be just as wrong not to fully utilize
the capacities of a well-built and intelligent horse
as to waste a weaker horse (physically or morally)
by excessive demands.

"And what about Laktišová?" you could ask me now. Some people are curious. Yes, what about Laktišová?

Laktišová, of course, is me. Since Flaubert was Madame Bovary, that shouldn't surprise anyone anymore. At least I don't have a mustache. After all, you shouldn't attach too much importance to it, because in this story, if it is one, when you see a sparrow fly past or a bus drive by noisily (one of the new ones, with square windows, forty-four seats, and twenty-six standing places) that will be me too. In this story, if it is one, without me and the wind not a single leaf can flutter.

After the bus has noisily crossed this story, gone around the square, and stopped without anyone getting off, Laktišová will feel her knees bend. In fact, people got off, let's say, at random, three little old ladies in floral-print jackets and big skirts, or the man in the blue suit with the big black briefcase, but they don't matter for Laktišová at this moment; for her—what an ability of simplifying the world!—no one got off. And her knees: bang! You know the feeling when the doctor hits your patella with a little hammer, and your leg jumps up all by itself without asking permission. This declaration of independence is so unexpected that Laktišová prefers to sit down on a bench, because what if her legs ever just decided to leave? She's sitting on the bench (behind her, the terrace of a café, where a brunette waitress is making a young Gypsy boy pay for his long night) and watching the bus through her big sunglasses in the hope that someone will get off anyway. Nobody gets off. No. Nobody's going to get off. For Laktišová, it's only a brief moment of weakness; she gets up quickly and her knees—after all (*Laktišová, c'est moi*), they're my knees, so let's not get too excited about them— obey her again, and she heads toward the post office to put her world back in order. She requests an intercity toll call, and a few moments later, she has Someone on the other end. "I can't come. It's really not possible," etc. A feeling of injustice falls on Laktišová like a suitcase falling from the baggage rack; she's incapable of saying a word, she only swallows her tears, but not all of them, two or three roll out from behind her sunglasses and stop on her cheeks, copious and bulbous, with the little shining window of the reflection of light. She sits down on the massive wooden bench next to the wall and when she lifts her sunglasses to wipe away her tears, she perceives a young pregnant woman in a black dress sitting next to her. The woman is evidently waiting for an intercity call, and to pass the time, she presses her chin against her hands and sobs loudly; no, not loudly, because you can't hear anything, but in a visible way: her head jumps back and forth as if someone is pulling her hair. Some people, faced with such obvious and genuine unhappiness, would be ashamed of their artificial pain, of their little bastard sorrow, but not Laktišová. Fresh, pulpy tears replace those that she has wiped away, and the two women stay seated next to each other, one pregnant and dressed in black, her head leaning forward, jumping to the rhythm of hiccups, and the other, with a red nose, her sunglasses pushed up on her forehead like a notary and with big transparent tears on her cheeks. One might say that they were fraternally sharing in the same crying, as if they produced it in concert, each with her own phase. That geometrically pure, linearly delimited space has so much intimate heat and defenselessly trickling mucus that a mustached old man, as dried-out as a prune (you may have guessed that it's the Transcarpathian process in retirement who, now having all his time to himself, can show the better side of his character), can't refrain from saying to them:

EVER GREEN IS . . .

180
▼

"Don't cry, girls. What good is crying? We all have to pass away. But you're still alive and young, so don't cry. Look at me; soon it will be my turn, but I'm not crying."

Encouraging words. Indeed, Laktišová (completely me!), as if she had been waiting for such a fairy-tale grandfather, rapidly wiped the steam of sentimentality that had condensed on the clear windowpane of the day with the sleeve of her floral-print blouse, and told herself that in fact, who gives a damn about Someone and all the external, bus-imported sorrows! She would have even laughed, but she was afraid (here being drags its feet a little behind consciousness) that a bubble might burst out of her nose.

And so much for Laktišová.

25

> An intelligent rider foresees the expected struggle
> and eventually takes measures to prevent the
> struggle. But if the struggle turns out to be
> inevitable, rider, use all of your force and will-
> power and fight to the end, fight for hours
> if need be, but do not give up! Carry out your
> fight to the bitter end with every kind of trick
> and have no mercy!

When we had finished eating, Mother put all of the dishes in the sink and said: "I think I'll take a little nap. Would you like to lie down for a little while yourself?" Half an hour later, I went softly into her bedroom. I had the impression that Mother was sleeping, although she wasn't breathing very deeply. I couldn't be sure, because it wouldn't have been the first time she had fooled us out of kindness or cunning; out of kindness was easily understandable: she wanted to make us happy and give us a moment of respite; but out of cunning—I had a little trouble explaining that to myself. Was it a kind of game with tacit rules, which we had started playing without realizing we were in it? Or did she perhaps want to impose her will even at the price of a trick? I was quite convinced that she was sleeping; but I wasn't trying to make my task easier. In any case, she wasn't expecting what was coming, and those were the stakes. I knew that as soon as I began, I wouldn't back down, because how could I let my mother live with the knowledge that her own son had tried to suffocate her with a pillow, and on top of that—it's this, I think, that she would have found most difficult to bear—he was such a klutz that he couldn't even pull it off. Mothers are equipped, it's true, with an unlimited imagination for excusing their children, but this would have required good psychological health and a spirit flexible enough to bounce back from reality like a ball; a tired person is left to fall prey to the truth—she doesn't have the strength to dodge its arrows nor to quickly find the word that could soften its rough edges a bit.

I went into the next room to look for the big pillow. The parquet floor creaked under the carpet, the door of the wardrobe creaked too, but I willingly accepted that test: If she was going to wake up, then have her wake up right away. Then I sat down for a moment on the chair next to the bed. Mother was breathing so peacefully that I had to lean over to see against the wall whether her duvet was moving, but her face was not calm and relaxed; she was frowning as if sleep required a great effort from her. I watched her . . . yes, almost avidly; I was forcing myself to decipher another face in that face, a face of times past, let's say, at least seven, or—I was progressively backing down—maybe five years ago. No, I could not. In the past, I would have been able to. But not now. I watched her because I wanted to engrave her image on my memory, and I engraved it. Then I took the pillow by both ends—I didn't want to push my hands directly on her face, so I wouldn't leave fingerprints—and I pushed.

I was surprised to see that her body clung so little to life. I was expecting something worse. Of course, of course, there were a few movements, but . . . aimless, without a common goal or denominator. Nothing that resembled a struggle. She hardly lifted her hands—and how afraid I had been to be scratched!—from the duvet. Even the groans under the pillow were stifled, as if she were swallowing a bit noisily, nothing more. There was nothing but a jolt: just before the end, she arched her back a bit . . . this movement of her hips seemed obscene to me, and that annoyed me because I had wanted her to part in total dignity. First I was annoyed by her, and then I was annoyed that, at a moment like that, I had found something physical obscene. But at the same time, I told myself: Better me than someone else! Funny ideas. I wasn't prepared for that.

She certainly didn't have time to understand what was happening to her. It was nothing but a rapid passage from the night of sleep to the night under the pillow. To the ultimate night beyond the pillow. That was the goal. I'm not very demanding; a man eventually learns to accept compromises.

Suddenly I heard a fly buzz and then I noticed the silence. A fly wouldn't have surprised me in the kitchen, but in the bedroom . . . I had forgotten to close the door. The idea that a fly could stay in the same room as the corpse made me feel sick—as if it could accelerate the decomposition process or something like that. I went to the window to shoo it outside when I heard in my head, like a third party talking about me, the phrase "He wouldn't hurt a fly." I laughed in my heart of hearts (it was such an angry laugh) and I crushed the stupid fly. It left a greasy streak on the windowpane. Mother wouldn't have liked that; a lot of strangers would be coming now, so I spat on my finger and wiped away the trace.

When I lifted the pillow . . . I don't know why I felt this, but I went into the bathroom, got a damp handkerchief, and wiped Mother's face. I felt a great tenderness for her; maybe such a movement, such a handmade kindness produces tenderness by itself . . . or maybe a suitable moment for tenderness came at last. I still wasn't able to imagine her younger, but that wasn't important; at that moment, her face was . . . not irrelevant, but beyond time. It wouldn't have even bothered me if she had suddenly sprouted whiskers.

I remember that when I was a child, I often asked the question: How is it possible that Mother goes to the dentist and I don't feel any pain? For me, it was as if I had caught myself in the act of lying. It called human relations into question. If my teeth didn't ache, it meant I didn't love her. So what a monster I was! Didn't I love my mother? A child's reflections. But in fact: How was it possible that a person could suddenly find himself alone during an attack of nephritic colic? How can we tolerate this? The Indian men who twist themselves and groan during the pains of childbirth, while their wives give birth in silence, are certainly strange, but I can understand their actions.

This is what I was thinking as I waited for the ambulance. How can we admit that someone finds herself alone at the moment of death? Of course, we can be sitting next to her bed, but that doesn't change anything: we're sitting next to her bed, but it's she who is dying. The gulf between us isn't reduced for all that. In contrast, I felt the harmony, the logical beauty—if such a thing exists—of the event that had just happened: we had shared the same experience, although I had been, let's say, heads, and she had been tails. We had been very close at that moment, right next to each other, on opposite sides of the same experience. Something like that.

"I see that you applied cold compresses on her," the doctor said, as she unbuttoned Mother's nightgown.

"I tried; I thought that it was going to ease her pain."

She didn't say anything, she just smiled, half tenderly and half condescendingly; I don't know what she looked like, or even if she was old or young, but I'd still be able to draw that smile.

"It must have been at least two hours ago," said the nurse, or perhaps he was the driver; in any case, a specialist. I had also realized that spots were already beginning to appear on Mother's left cheek and the left side of her nose. I must have pressed hard there without knowing it.

"I thought she was sleeping," I said. "I didn't want to wake her."

They didn't stay long. Before leaving the room, the doctor leaned over Mother and, more like a woman than a doctor, she closed Mother's eyes. In fact, I hadn't thought of that myself. I felt that, despite her professional savoir faire, it was a gesture full of tenderness, a caress from the end of her finger, as if making the sign of the cross on someone's forehead before he sets off on a long journey. The act itself didn't have much meaning, because the forensic surgeon, who arrived about two hours later, reopened her eyes for his examination. He looked at her throat and her chest, he read the exit protocol from the hospital and filled out the death certificate (cause of death: cardiac arrest).

"It's clear for me. But if you'd like us to do an autopsy . . ."

I shrugged. "If it's not necessary, why bother."

"You can go with this document to the undertaker's," he told me. "You should also take her identity card and a pension form. They'll take care of the rest." And as he went out the door, he added, "It would be better to dress her right away, before she gets stiff."

It's interesting that all this time, I didn't feel any tension, I wasn't afraid that the doctor or the surgeon would discover something; it wasn't that I hadn't imagined such a possibility, but it didn't matter to me. I won't bargain where my mother is concerned. It was only as I was dressing Mother, at the moment when I was trying to sit her up and a little air came out of her compressed lungs, that I had a little fright: I had the impression that after that heavy sigh, she was going to open her eyes, and say, searching with difficulty for ordinary human words, as she did every time she woke up: "I had such a funny nightmare."

Around six o'clock, two men came from the undertaker's, carrying (in accordance with the order) a coffin of imitation black marble without a lid, and softly, carefully, lifted Mother from the bed. I opened the door to the stairs for them and said, "See you." "Good-bye," they responded. At first, I was shocked by their words, but they were right. Professionals. What good were threats? I looked out the window as they were putting the coffin in the car; at that moment, as they say, I saw Mother for the last time. What a load of bull.

At the back of the kitchen cupboard—my nose hadn't fooled me—I found an open bottle of Romanian cognac. I carried it into the bedroom. It was the bedroom—no, I had to lift up the duvet and the sheet again—that I had known since my childhood. Usually, that inertia of things, that stubborn persistence, irritated me, but here it rather delighted me. As if the bedroom, by its immutability, wanted to assure me that nothing had happened. I filled a glass and, sitting down comfortably in the armchair, I drank with a certain pleasure. Yes, everything was in its place: the bookshelf, the couch, the big table with its chairs, the armchairs, the wardrobe, and even the pictures on the wall . . . and Mother bustling about in the kitchen. I didn't see her, but I knew she was in the kitchen. When I had finished drinking, I would go out to see her.

Suddenly, still sitting with the glass in my hand, I remembered something absurd: absurd, because it went against all logic, but that was exactly why I was convinced that I hadn't invented it. I don't have such a fertile imagination. It was a brief, sunny apparition: Mother, dressed in a flower-print dress, was sitting in the middle of a meadow, laughing freely, surrounded by baby geese that, probably confused by the design, were attacking her dress with their beaks. Mother (and wasn't she always so attentive to her things!) is letting them do it; she keeps on laughing and watches as her beautiful clothing is reduced to rags. I leap about in the meadow with a heavy wooden sword in my hand. The meadow is big, endless, we're alone there, Mother, me, and the goslings. The goslings are stupid, yellow, and clumsy. Mother is young and happy.

At last. Now everything is truly in its place. The horse upstairs, the blind man in Vráble.

Any other questions, Beverley?

Everything I Know about Central Europeanism

4   *Jean Genet*

Genet actually lived in Brno for several months in 1937, and he mentions his Moravian experiences in *The Thief's Journal* (1949).

11   *another European writer*

The writer referred to is the Moravian dissident Ludvik Vaculik; the quotation comes from his best-known work, *The Czech Dream-Book* (*Český snář*, 1980).

12   *"It's true that . . ."*

This excerpt comes from the first chapter of Camus's 1947 novel *The Plague.*

Ever Green Is . . .

13   *Colonel Alfredl*

Alfredl is a thinly fictionalized version of Colonel Alfred Redl, a high-ranking Habsburg officer who committed suicide in 1913 after his espionage activities (and homosexual affairs) were discovered. Redl was also the subject of Istvan Szabo's film *Colonel Redl.*

13   *K.u.K.*

This abbreviation for *kaiserlich und königlich,* "Imperial-Royal," was historically used for the Austro-Hungarian Empire (which Robert Musil referred to as "Kakania"). In this case, however, "K.u.K." is also Colonel Alfredl's code name (something like James Bond's use of "007").

20   *Hazi Schwarzwald Sextett*

According to the author, this imaginary character was named after the Hazy Osterwald Sextet, a Swiss jazz group whose music was played on Austrian radio in the 1940s and 1950s.

23   *well-known historical figure*

The narrator is referring to Hitler, who wrote his infamous *Mein Kampf* while imprisoned for treason in 1924. (While of course primarily anti-Semitic, *Mein Kampf* also contains passages condemning the Slavs, particularly the Czechs.) In the 1920s, the influential "psychic" Erik Jan Hanussen gave Hitler lessons in public speaking.

36   *alienation*

This is a parody of the line "When I hear the word 'culture,' I reach for my Browning!" which is often attributed to the Nazi leader Hermann Göring.

49   *"Csak egy kis emlék"*

As Slovak readers would probably recognize, the Romanian chambermaid is actually speaking Hungarian, demonstrating the overlapping nature of Central European national identities.

72   *Yehiel Blum*

The character Blum/Stummdorfer-Wisniewsky, like Hazi Schwarzwald Sextett, is based purely on wordplay. In this case, the irony lies in the way that Central

European surnames (as well as place names, such as Pressburg/Pozony/Bratislava) were frequently changed along with political regimes.

82   *Štefánik*

Milan Rastislav Štefánik (1880–1919) was an astronomer, politician, and general in the French army who became the leading Slovak member of the Czechoslovak liberation movement during World War I. He was killed in a plane crash near Bratislava shortly after the war (under what some considered suspicious circumstances) and became immortalized as a national hero.

83   *"Flagras fajro . . ."*

These lines are taken from an Esperanto version of Ján Botto's 1862 poem "The Death of Janošik." In English, the first stanza reads:

> *The little fire burns, it burns on the King's Mountain.*
> *Who started it?—Twelve falcons.*
> *Twelve falcons, white falcons*
> *Such as human eyes have never seen.*

The poem describes the fate of the semimythical bandit Juraj Janošik (1688–1713), Slovakia's national hero. Esperanto (perhaps the best-known artificial language) was created in Poland and has always had a devoted following in Central Europe.

91   *Si non è vero*

This saying (in modern Italian, not Latin) serves as a suitable motto for the narrator (as well as for translators): "Even if it's not true, it's well put."

92   *Karl May*

May (1842–1912) was a German novelist whose adventure stories, set in such places as the Wild West and the Middle East, are little known in the United

States but have remained extremely popular across Central Europe. Winnetou and Old Shatterhand appear in May's *Winnetou* (1893), which has been translated into English.

95 *Czech-to-Slovak dictionary*

This was one of the most challenging passages of the book to translate, since the original exploits the subtle but substantial variations between Czech and Slovak to comic effect. (Although the narrator is posing as a Czech tourist trying to speak Slovak, the text hints that neither Czech nor Slovak is his native language.) I decided to replace the Czech-Slovak distinction with British versus American English, a difference which Czech and Slovak dictionaries of English usually try to clarify, not always accurately.

102 *Baksheesh! Pengö! Korunky! Lóve! Das Geld!*

The cowherdess uses the Hungarian, Czech/Slovak, Romany, and German terms for money.

105 *Kollár*

The quotation on "freedom" comes from the prelude to *The Daughter of Slava* (1824) by Ján Kollár (1793–1852), the only major poet widely accepted as both a Czech and a Slovak writer.

111 *"ever green is . . ."*

This is a parody of Goethe's well-known line from *Faust:* "Grey is theory and ever green is the tree of life." The "green horse" may refer to Marcel Aymé's 1933 novel *The Green Mare,* a somewhat magical-realist family saga that was popular in Czechoslovakia in the 1960s.

A Horse Upstairs, a Blind Man in Vráble

121   *Galileo*

After being forced to revoke his claim that the earth revolves around the sun, Galileo made the famous statement, "*Eppur si muove*" ("It does move, though").

154   *colt of personality*

The pun here (unintentional on the mother's part) is of course on the infamous "cult of personality."

Pavel Vilikovský published his first collection of stories in 1965 and has published numerous other works in his native Slovakia. In 1997 Vilikovský won the Vilenica Award for Central European literature.

■ □ ■ □ ■

WRITINGS FROM AN UNBOUND EUROPE

Bait
Tsing
Words Are Something Else
DAVID ALBAHARI

City of Ash
EUGENIJUS ALIŠANKA

Skinswaps
ANDREJ BLATNIK

My Family's Role in the World Revolution and Other Prose
BORA ĆOSIĆ

Peltse and Pentameron
VOLODYMYR DIBROVA

The Victory
HENRYK GRYNBERG

The Tango Player
CHRISTOPH HEIN

A Bohemian Youth
JOSEF HIRŠAL

Charon's Ferry
GYULA ILLYÉS

Mocking Desire
Northern Lights
DRAGO JANČAR

Balkan Blues: Writing Out of Yugoslavia
JOANNA LABON, ED.

The Loss
VLADIMIR MAKANIN